A HEARSE FOR McNALLY

Gerry Westmayne had worked out how to steal the State Jewels of Lahkpore. McNally carried out the plan but, with cracksman Herb Setters, he stole the loot from Westmayne's safe only to discover that it was worthless. McNally had been outsmarted, and he began to wonder if he could trust Gilda Kemp. And after killing his boss he realized the extent of his girlfriend's treachery and learned too late the high cost of a place in the sun.

Books by G. J. Barrett
in the Linford Mystery Library:

MURDER ROAD

G. J. BARRETT

A HEARSE FOR McNALLY

Complete and Unabridged

LINFORD
Leicester

First published in Great Britain by
Robert Hale Limited
London

First Linford Edition
published 2005
by arrangement with
Robert Hale Limited
London

British Library CIP Data

Barrett, G. J.
 A hearse for McNally.—Large print ed.—
 Linford mystery library
 1. Detective and mystery stories
 2. Large type books
 I. Title
 823.9'14 [F]

 ISBN 1–84617–110–5

Published by
F. A. Thorpe (Publishing)
Anstey, Leicestershire

Set by Words & Graphics Ltd.
Anstey, Leicestershire
Printed and bound in Great Britain by
T. J. International Ltd., Padstow, Cornwall

1

Dave McNally kept digging steadily. The depth of the trench beneath him hardly seemed to increase at all. The blade of his shovel cut and chopped, then scraped forward and scooped, and he swung another thin shower of dirt on to the pile of earth by his left elbow. He brushed his sweating brow across a rolled shirtsleeve. His nerves were buzzing, and his head ached. The urge to work like a maniac took hold of him: to force his body to the limit of endurance; but he controlled the semi-hysterical impulse. Men didn't work as if their lives depended on it in these times. Before everything else, he had to look like an ordinary working man who was labouring just hard enough to uncover the gas service pipe that ran somewhere beneath his feet.

Forcing himself to rest, he straightened his back and gazed a short distance down the road. By the opposite curb, he saw

Fred Golson pulling the green canvas work-shelter out of the back of their 'borrowed' Gas Board van. The paunchy Fred looked as placid and unworried as a child at a picnic. He possessed the perfect temperament for a thief. Nerves he knew nothing about, his imagination was limited, and insecurity was a word unknown to him. He would go on whistling the Twelfth Street Rag with every policeman in the United Kingdom breathing down his neck.

'What's the time, Fred?' McNally called.

'Time you had that job done, mate,' came the reply.

'How would you like a kick up the backside?' McNally asked sweetly.

Golson grinned, but otherwise ignored the question. He set the work-shelter down on the road beside him. Then he bent into the back of the van again. He reappeared holding up a jacket by its collar. Dipping inside the garment, he brought out a pocket-watch. 'Just one o'clock,' he announced, turning the timepiece away from the brightest of the sunlight. 'Supposing you get on with it.'

'Belt up!' McNally advised. 'Supposing you get that shelter over here.'

Golson put both his jacket and the watch out of sight again. 'That's right. I can do two jobs at once, but you can't do even one.'

McNally nodded absently. He resumed digging, and didn't look up again. It was one thing to play a part, but quite another to waste time which they couldn't afford. He worked a little harder to make up for the lost minute. His mind was filled by the image of the semi-oriental façade of the Eastport Sporting Club, a building which stood only just beyond the shrubbery behind the van. He had about three quarters of an hour in which to plunge the great establishment, its racecourse, staff, officials, and the public who were already gathering in the main stand and along the home straight rails, into bewilderment and confusion. It wouldn't be difficult; the process had its precedent.

Since the 16th of July 1953, the day of the Francasal affair, no racecourse in the country had been free of the fear that somebody might try to repeat the betting coup that had so nearly come off at Bath. It would be necessary only for the telephone lines to go dead about half an hour before the 2.15 p.m. race — around the time when reports had just started coming in of unexpectedly heavy off course betting on 12 to 1 Merry Morn — and the band would start to play. And what a hullabaloo there would be when Rikeman Trunch discovered, as he soon must, that Joe Reith, his new head boy, had substituted Sister Sue, Merry Morn's equine double, as the runner for the Hatherly Stables in the 2.15. The 'evidence' would all be there; it had been fixed to the last detail. Trunch would find the pirate horse transporter, which had brought the second horse to Eastport, in a not too accessible part of the Sporting Club's grounds, brown dye that had been used to darken a light patch on one of Sister Sue's fetlocks would be discovered near the vehicle, and Reith himself would have disappeared. These things would cause the stewards to panic; the racecourse manager would get into touch

4

with the police; and the coppers, on locating the severed cable near the gas service pipe, would call in their best men and concentrate everything on the case. After that, the ground would be clear to put the more important part of Gerry Westmayne's plan for the afternoon into action. McNally smiled to himself. Westmayne knew his stuff all right, but he didn't know his men. For instance, he didn't know that McNally had a plan of his own — one that even Fred Golson didn't know about.

'Hot, boy?' Golson asked, dragging the work-shelter up to the hole and releasing it. He squinted upwards at the August sun that rode high and flaring near the cloudless blue of the midheaven. 'Who'd be a fried egg?'

'Stinker!' McNally jeered. 'I'd forgotten digging was such hard work. Come and have a try.'

Golson yawned. 'What me in my state of health? You must be joking. I'm the foreman.' Grunting, he squatted and peered into the trench, picking up earth and letting it sift through his fingers as he did so. 'The pipe is down at three feet six according to the plan. You ought to reach it before long.'

'You know damn well it's not the pipe I want to see,' McNally retorted, throwing down his shovel and tugging his shirt over his head. 'Here.' He passed his shirt up to his stout companion, and picked up the shovel again, muscles rippling in his powerful arms and torso as he went back to work with much of the fierce zeal that he had been trying to avoid a short time ago.

'Whoa, Liza!' Golson warned. 'You be careful you don't put your shovel through that bloody cable. You know what plans are. You don't want to end up strumming a harp on cloud nine.'

'Why not?' McNally asked caustically. 'I'm a noble soul.'

Golson gave vent to a rattling laugh. 'Some hopes! You're okay now. The cable should be over to the right, and an inch or two deeper.'

'I've seen the plans too,' McNally panted. 'Get ready to push the shelter over me. You can never tell who's going to miss the Sporting Club turn and come nosing into this cul-de-sac.'

'True enough, boy,' Golson admitted. 'The less anybody sees, the better. But I don't think you're going to need it all that much. The real job will only take a minute.'

'Me with an oxy-acetylene torch in full view!' McNally exclaimed. 'Come off it, Fred!'

Golson laughed good-naturedly, and rocked on his heels, his belly folding and unfolding between his thighs. 'Butter-flies?' he asked seriously.

'No time for 'em,' McNally lied.

'Says he!' Golson retorted.

'So what?'

'Nothing. Being a bit sick in the gut is part of the price.'

'Of what?'

'Getting taken suddenly rich. West-mayne said a cool quarter million, didn't he?'

'A hot one,' McNally corrected, cursing the longhaired blonde wig which he wore for the purposes of the day over his own short brown hair. The thing irritated horribly in the heat, as did the wispy moustaches that hung at either corner of his mouth. But the disguise was necessary; he had no doubts about that. His bright-eyed, clean-cut good looks were of the immediately recognizable sort. There were watchers everywhere. You didn't realize how many until you started breaking the law.

'I'm going to buy up a boozer and drown myself in best bitter,' Golson said ecstatically.

'Don't start counting your chickens, Fred,' McNally warned abruptly; 'it breaks your concentration. Once that's gone, you're done for!'

The shovel went on chunking and thudding and scraping. Time passed. The pile of soil beside McNally now grew appreciably.

'There's the gas pipe,' Golson said, pointing excitedly as an inch or two of corroded piping showed through the damp soil at the bottom of the trench.

McNally nodded. Then he shifted his attention to the right of his metal guide and eased the dirt away in caked layers until the heavy insulation of an electric cable came into view. Glancing up, he grinned briefly, shook the sweat off his face, and sent his shovel spearing across the path at Golson's side. 'That does it, Fred. What's the time now?'

'Eh?'

'Where's your watch?'

'You'll make me thin,' Golson said indignantly, leaving the trench and walking back to the van, then returning with the watch in his hand. 'Twenty-seven minutes past. That isn't bad.'

'It's good mate. Too good.'

'You don't have to be too exact, surely?'

'You know what Westmayne is. He said a quarter to. Let's be having the tent.'

Golson slipped the watch into his back pocket, then pushed the canvas work-shelter over the trench. McNally's face dimmed to an ivory facsimile in the shadow that settled about him.

'Want me to fetch the things over?' Golson asked, wheezing slightly from the effort.

'Relax,' McNally advised, climbing out of the trench and scratching the mud off the knees of his denim overall trousers. 'Let's have a smoke.'

'You're getting brave,' Golson yawned.

'I've got to be.'

'And so obedient.'

'Ha, bloody, ha!' McNally walked over to an iron fence adjacent, and lifted his jacket off a spike. From one of the pockets he took twenty cigarettes. Opening the packet, he offered one to his companion. Golson took it, flipped the filtered tip between his lips, and supplied a match. Their cigarettes burning, they leaned against the fence and inhaled enjoyably.

McNally glanced sideways at Golson. The fat man looked three parts asleep. How relaxed could you get? Then McNally scowled to himself. Golson's remark about his growing too obedient had stung. He didn't like anybody to impugn his courage or independence of spirit. If only the fat man knew what was coming. But Golson must never know. The McNally secret must rest between McNally and Herb Setters for as long as they lived. But he didn't have to worry about Herb. Herb was a true blue professional; about the best screwsman in the business. When he and Setters had done what they planned, they would disappear: leave East Anglia for ever. The world was large, and it had wonderful things to offer the man with money. For a moment McNally fell into the trap of counting his chickens. Then he thought of Gilda Kemp. Without Gilda, there would be no point in any of what he must go through today. He would take Gilda with him. She was the best of the things that money could buy him. He sighed out a deep inhalation of smoke. The minutes went by. Then he glanced at Golson again and said: 'Kiaora?'

'You'll mess yourself,' Golson growled, digging out his watch again. 'Twenty-four minutes to two. Want me to bring the bottle and burner over now?'

'Yes.' McNally watched Golson move unhurriedly towards the van. Then he saw the other crane towards the open end of the cul-de-sac, lose colour, and shudder visibly. McNally jerked his own head round. He saw at once the reason for

Golson's disturbance. There was a policeman sauntering along the nearby street. The copper was a huge fellow, not less than six feet four inches tall, of more than proportionately broad and heavy build, with straight, stern features, intolerant eyes, and a magnificent 'handlebar' moustache. His presence was tremendous. He seemed to carry the full majesty of the law with him. No more daunting figure could possibly have appeared in the vicinity at that moment. 'Steady!' breathed McNally; but the briefly shaken Golson was already sauntering back towards him and whistling as if he hadn't got a care in the world.

Just then the policeman's gaze turned into the cul-de-sac. His eyes met McNally's. Curiosity showed in them, but no suspicion. Still looking, the constable walked slowly across the gap, then turned his head to the front again and vanished behind an overhanging hedge at the corner of the continuation of the street which he was patrolling. 'Hold it!' McNally urged, as Golson appeared about to turn again. 'I've got an idea he'll be back. If he does, we'll be at work.'

Picking up his shovel, McNally got down into the trench again and watched the front of the cul-de-sac. Sure enough, the policeman reappeared in less than a minute. He turned into the opening and strode ponderously towards the work-shelter. 'What were you two up to?' he asked stonily, stopping beside the heap of excavated soil.

'Having a fag,' McNally replied, grinning.

'Gas men?' the officer accused.

'Safe enough. We were well clear.'

'You must know,' the other agreed doubtfully. 'On overtime, then?'

'Overtime?' McNally rubbed his face to hide the fact that he had been taken aback. 'Oh, ah. Every little helps, as the old woman said. I don't care for this Saturday lark, though. But a job came in, and the office hooked me and my mate out. It's too urgent to let slide over the weekend.'

The constable nodded stolidly. 'What's wrong?'

'The trouble's in the staff flats behind

the Sporting Club,' McNally replied glibly. 'The tenants have complained of loss of pressure. Me and my mate measured at just about zero to the square inch. That's no good to anybody. We've found a leak in the service pipe.'

The policeman sniffed. 'I don't smell gas,' he remarked.

'You wouldn't. We've turned it off along here.'

'I see.'

'We want to get the job done smartish,' McNally hinted. 'I promised the wife and nipper an afternoon on the Keystone Pier. But I expect they'll have to make the best of the evening instead. Pity to waste all this sun, sweating.'

The constable grunted noncommittally.

McNally turned and bent over the pipe. He felt the officer's eyes on his back. Why couldn't the big goof get the message and go away? A typical example, no doubt, of too much beef and too little under the helmet. Big men were almost all the same. It was no good, the so-and-so seemed to have become a fixture. A bit more boring conversation

14

might break his inertia. It was worth trying anyway. 'Plenty doing at the racecourse today,' he called up between his legs. 'Good card, so they tell me. There'll be plenty of louts around. I bet they'll give you plenty to do.'

'I'm not worrying,' the officer replied. 'What are you going to do?'

'Down here?' McNally had been caught off guard a second time. 'Oh, replace a section of the pipe.' He thumped his shovel into the soil, then began an energetic scraping around. Would the big varmint never go? The minutes were ticking away. It must be almost a quarter to two. If Westmayne's ruse were to fully succeed, the telephone cable must be cut as soon after the quarter as possible.

The policeman moved. Hands behind his back, he circled the trench, then stopped again at the door of the work-shelter and thrust his head inside. 'What's that?' he asked, pointing at the cable with a finger about the size of a carrot.

'The opposition,' McNally replied,

striving to keep a note of anger and anxiety out of his voice.

'Who?'

'The Electricity Board.'

'Um.' The officer appeared to surprise himself as much as his informant with a brief chuckle. 'Still, gas from coal has about had it.'

'Not on your nelly!' McNally declared in indignant loyalty. 'Our retorts will be full for many a day yet. We've got the measure of the lot at the power station — and the blokes out on the rigs. We're far cheaper all round!'

'I'm all for that,' the policeman said, his interest dissolving into indifference. Slowly, he turned back a cuff and looked at his wristwatch; then, raising a bushy eyebrow, he screwed round on his heel and moved towards the street, nodding to Golson, who had kept well back and remained the silent onlooker, as he went.

McNally watched the giant officer out of the cul-de-sac, then twisted his head towards his fat helper and snapped: 'Hurry, hurry, hurry, Fred! I hope his old woman feeds him Rodine for strawberry jam!'

Golson lumbered over to the van. The vehicle trembled slightly as he moved heavy equipment about in the back of it. Then he reappeared with a small steel cylinder under one arm, and a blowtorch attached to a length of tubing under the other. Kneeling at the edge of the trench, he lowered the cylinder to the ground and passed the torch down to McNally, who opened its valve and put a match to the escaping gas, then adjusted the flame until it was a searing point of bluish-white light in the sunshine that reached the upper levels of the shadow in which the hole was immersed.

'Here you are,' Golson panted, handing down a pair of welding goggles. 'It's ten minutes to two. Not so lucky, are we?'

'A proper muck up!' McNally agreed, putting on the goggles and bending towards the cable with the blowtorch held in front of him. The flame touched the insulation; plastic oozed, and rubber stank; then the wires beneath began to spit and splutter, and blue sparks jumped.

In another moment, the cable was totally severed and, shutting off the blowtorch, McNally threw it out of the trench and hopped up after it. 'Gather the stuff!' he ordered. 'If anybody from the Sporting Club has seen us at work here, they could be getting ideas at this very moment.' He picked up his shovel, grabbed a pick that he had used earlier, and plucked his jacket off the fence. 'Ready?' he demanded.

'Have been ever since we got here,' Golson retorted.

They ran to the van. Golson tossed the cylinder and blowtorch into the back, and McNally threw the tools and his jacket on top of them. Then he slammed and fastened the rear doors, dived along the side of the vehicle, and tumbled in behind the wheel. He pressed the starter and slipped into gear as Golson thumped down on the seat beside him. 'What about the work-shelter?' the fat man inquired, his voice pitched an octave higher than usual.

'Leave it!' McNally snapped, letting in the clutch and rolling to the mouth of the cul-de-sac, where he hung momentarily to look left and right before accelerating into a left turn and punishing the gearbox as he picked up the higher gears many revs before they were ready to engage. He kept his eyes darting into either wing mirror, but saw no signs of a pursuit. Equally, there was nobody on the street who showed the smallest interest in the van. McNally let his shoulders slump a little as some of his tension drained away.

'I wish we hadn't left it behind,' Golson mused, his teeth gritting softly.

'What?' McNally asked sharply, dropping into third and turning right at an intersection. 'Are you still on about the shelter?'

'Dabs.'

'We've both got a clean bill of health,' McNally retorted. 'That thing must be smothered in fingerprints. Where's the worry?'

'I don't like leaving dabs behind,' Golson said stubbornly. 'It isn't professional. Westmayne would crucify us.'

'Westmayne saves the nice jobs for himself,' McNally sneered. 'Cut it out,

Fred; it isn't like you.'

Golson's lips compressed tightly; then he said: 'You're not as good as you think, Dave.'

'Who said I was perfect?' McNally asked, giving a short, contemptuous laugh.

'You think — '

'Stow it, Fred! We can't afford to start quarrelling now. If you must have a row, come and see me tonight, when the work's behind us, and you can curse and call me all you want — and I'll curse and call you. Right?'

Golson didn't answer. He jogged McNally's arm. 'Look! There's that great lump of a copper again!'

McNally turned his gaze in the direction indicated by his companion's nodding jaw. He saw the policeman on his left, standing near the curb and beside a pillar box. The officer looked bigger, sterner, and more intolerant than ever. His eyes came to rest on the van and its occupants. A question took form in them and hardened. Now the man was suspicious. McNally swore under his breath. He had been careless. He ought to have considered the presence of the policeman in the area and left the cul-de-sac by a more circuitous route. But it was much too late for regrets now. He leaned sideways to pick up the constable's reflection in the nearside mirror, and saw Golson craning at the window. 'What's he doing?' McNally demanded.

'He's getting his notebook out.'

'I can see him now. He's got our number.'

'Is he on walkie-talkie?'

'I didn't see anything like that on him. Don't blow it up too big, Fred. We're public servants.'

'What if he rings the office of the Gas Board?'

'Let him. We're only five minutes from putting this van back where it belongs. It would take a lot longer than that for the Gas Board — assuming there's anybody at their office on a Saturday afternoon — to look up the name and address of the driver of our van and get an inquiry started.'

'Let's play safe, and dump it.'

'There's no sense in that, Fred. Anywhere around here, we'd be vulnerable on foot. Remember, he saw us working, and the cut cable speaks for itself. It's as sure as anything can be this van is going to be identified as the one we used sooner or later. But that's all there is to it. What's the name of the Gas Board chap who drives it during the week? Ernie Watts, isn't it? Ernie doesn't know us from Adam, even when I'm out of this wig and 'tache. We're just two more faces seen through the bar-room smoke while he shoots his big mouth off in the Farrier's Arms. He won't have a clue when the bogies put him through their mincer. Let's make the best use we can of this old wreck. Okay?'

'Whatever you say, Dave,' Golson said resignedly.

McNally nodded confidently. Then they moved out of the modern residential area through which they had been passing and turned into narrower, smoke-darkened streets, where working-class houses, shell-like in their poverty, packed into blocks and grim terraces. In the background a gasometer loomed, and the cranes of the riverside dockland knelt above the rooftops on the left like so many huge and limbless grasshoppers. Cobbles bumped under the tyres, and the smell of drains entered at the window. McNally wrinkled his nose and pulled a face, then set his winkers flashing and turned into a narrow lane on the right that ran between high brick walls and finally issued on to an old bomb site, where the outlines of foundations were still visible through the dust. Swinging the van into a corner, where the blind walls of adjoining warehouses met, McNally brought it to a halt and switched off the engine. 'There you are,' he said, patting the wheel as he got out. 'Exactly as Ernie left it. How's the old kiaora now?'

'Two fifteen,' Golson answered. 'The race is about to start.'

'I wasn't thinking about that,' McNally said, striding away from the van. 'Come on, slow-coach! There's time for a pint before the Lord Nelson closes.'

They hurried to the opposite side of the bomb site, and left it by an alley that gave access to a street which ran more-or-less parallel with the river. With the odours of tar and salt and nitrates in their nostrils, they approached a corner where a jutting sign announced the presence of the Lord Nelson. 'So far so good,' Golson said, as they paused outside the door. 'May stage two go as well. My palms are itching!'

'We'll find you plenty to scratch them on,' McNally promised, slapping his shorter companion on the shoulder. 'Plenty!'

2

Detective Chief Inspector John Blessingay was feeling distinctly smug. He had managed it at last; an afternoon off. He raised his slippered feet to the mantel-piece, tucked his favourite briar into the corner of his mouth, opened Tolstoy's Resurrection at the marked page, and sighed contentedly as he listened to the first movement of Mozart's 'Jupiter' Symphony issuing from the stereogram. Leisure, he decided, with a wisdom not uninspired by a recent whisky, was appreciated and understood only by those who got very little of it. He could hear his wife in the next room, fussing about with a duster, but he had no intention of letting the sounds of her diligence disturb him. For the next few hours he meant to regale his soul with the world's greatest works of art. Nothing was going to interfere with this long planned and just as often postponed period of spiritual rejuvenation. Even a copper had the right to occasional glimpses of the sphere of wonder which lay behind the grim illusion that men called reality. Besides, he liked to be thoroughly lazy once in a while.

Pausing, he listened to the modulations which preceded the recapitulation of Mozart's first subject, blew out smoke and beat time with his pipe stem, sighed his appreciation, and then started reading in earnest. He had got through two sentences when the phone rang. He stiffened, his feet sliding into the hearth, and sat up apprehensively. He stared towards the hall; his sense of peace and contentment had vanished. The fragrant winds of the spirit had taken themselves elsewhere, and the familiar sourness of his professional outlook again soaked through the fibres of his mind. Surely it couldn't be what he feared. The Station couldn't be summoning him; there was an inspector on duty. Even policemen had some consideration for one another. Everybody at Boyne Street knew how thoroughly he deserved these few hours off. No, it couldn't be the Station calling. Probably one of his wife's friends was at the other end of the line. Of course, that would be bad enough. Joy's friends were such infernal chatterboxes.

Blessingay listened to his wife's footsteps approaching the phone on the hall table. He heard her lift the receiver and say 'hello'. Really, she had no sense of the instrument at all; so few people had. 'Yes,' she said, and 'No,' she said, and 'Oh, dear, must you;' and then she spoke the dreaded words 'Yes, I understand. I'll fetch him,' She meant 'call', obviously; just that little difference which meant so much. What a carping so-and-so he was when put out. Here came the footsteps again. They stopped outside the door. 'John!' his wife called tentatively.

'Yes?' He might as well humour her in their usual little ritual.

She opened the door and thrust a face still round and pretty into the room. 'I'm sorry, dear.'

He could see that she was sorry, too. 'The Station?'

'Yes.'

'What the dickens do they want?' he asked, his grumpiness coming through the serene resignation he had been determined to reflect.

'They want you to go in straight away. They didn't tell me any more than that.'

'They wouldn't,' he said with a deprecating sniff which still managed to convey his satisfaction that the proprieties had been correctly observed. He put his book aside, got to his feet, and stretched himself. 'I'll come and have a word with them.'

His wife opened the door wide, and he strode by her into the hall. Reaching the table, he picked up the telephone receiver which lay beside its rest and put it to his ear. 'Blessingay here,' he said.

Sergeant Logan answered him. The sergeant's voice was low-keyed and apologetic.

'You'd better make it good, Sergeant,' he warned.

'It is good, sir,' Logan replied.

'Where's Inspector Fisher? He's supposed to be in charge of C.I.D. this afternoon. Hell's bells, it is Saturday!'

'Inspector Fisher had an accident at lunchtime, sir.'

'An accident? What sort of accident?'

'Er, it happened when he was taking his dog for a walk, sir. He tripped over the lead, and sprained an ankle rather badly.'

'Some mothers have 'em!' Blessingay moaned. 'What's it all about?'

Logan paused. 'Excuse me, sir. The Deputy Chief Constable wants to speak to you.'

'Very good.' Blessingay cocked his chin and waited. This business must be really important. Albert Bryant didn't often put his oar in.

'John?' Bryant puffed as if he had indigestion.

'Sir.'

'I want you to come in right away.'

'I've been told.'

'Sorry. Do you remember the Francasal business at Bath back in '53?'

Blessingay wrinkled his brow. 'Yes, I remember, sir. Reg Spooner's big one — outside the murder cases, I mean.'

'That's right. It looks as if we've got a reissue on at the Sporting Club today.'

'What about that!' The chief inspector was impressed despite himself.

'Yes,' Albert Bryant went on. 'It appears things got started a little before two o'clock. The L.P.S.N.A. 'blower' service was sending in word of a lot of late heavy plunging on a horse in the 2.15 race. Merry Morn, a 12 to 1 outsider. It seems the wires suddenly went dead. All eight circuits packed up at the same moment.

'Running on a bit, the 2.15 race was run as per card, and Merry Morn won at a trot. Payment to winners has naturally been withheld.

'I understand that Allenby-Newton, the Sporting Club's manager, and the stewards, have already been busy. Doing some of our work for us, you might say. They've discovered a second horse on their property that's Merry Morn's double. This animal comes from the Hatherly Stables at Newmarket, which is also Merry Morn's home. What's equally important, they've found a hole dug in a cul-de-sac at the back of the Sporting Club's main building. At the bottom of the hole lies a severed cable. It's another blowtorch job. What do you think?'

'It sounds like an open and shut case,' Blessingay replied guardedly. 'Do they know who dug the hole, sir? I mean, was anybody seen at work in the cul-de-sac?'

'Sorry. I ought to have told you. The digging was done by a pair of phony Gas Board men.'

'That's all you know.'

'That's all, yes.'

'It's got betting coup written all over it.'

'So we all think. I've been in touch with the Chief Constable, John. He says we must treat it as such.'

'And I'm to take it from there?'

'Of course,' Bryant answered. 'It's too big for any of our lesser lights to handle. Er, John.'

'Sir?'

'Handle it discreetly, won't you? There are big names involved. For instance, the Hatherly Stables are owned by Rikeman Trunch, confidant of the nobility and friend of Royalty.'

'I'll do my best, sir,' Blessingay said rather stiffly, adding: 'Consistent with my duty and the law.'

'Naturally, John,' Bryant soothed. 'I may take it you're on your way, then?'

'Ten minutes, sir. Is Sergeant Logan still there?'

'Yes.' There was a faint sound, as of the receiver changing hands.

'Yes, sir?' Logan inquired.

'Be waiting for me at the Police Station door, Sergeant.'

'Very good, sir.'

Blessingay rattled the receiver back on to its rest. He kicked off his slippers, then picked them up and carried them to the corner at the end of the hall in which his shoes were standing. Dumping his slippers, he pulled on his shoes and laced them up, keeping a slanted eye on his wife all the time. 'No rest for the wicked,' he said, straightening his back with a grunt and giving his paunch a disciplinary slap.

'It's too bad, dear,' Joy Blessingay sympathized.

'So it is,' the chief inspector agreed, his mouth twisting into a wry smile. 'But it's my job and our living, you know. We can't fight that. Take the Mozart off, will you?

It's easy to muck up a diamond when a single-player runs out.'

'I'll see to it.'

'One of these days,' he said, moving to the peg on which his jacket was hanging, 'I'll hear the 'Jupiter' all through. Hey ho for black Saturday!'

'Weekends are always the worst,' his wife observed.

Blessingay slipped his jacket on and buttoned it. 'For me and a few thousand other coppers, eh? Give us a kiss.'

Mrs. Blessingay proffered her lips. He pecked at them, smiled into her eyes, squeezed her shoulder, and strode to the front door, putting on his Homburg as he went. Outside the house, he turned left to where his battered old Citroen stood in front of the garage, got in, started up, and drove the car down the short driveway to the front gate, where he made a right turn on to the main road and headed for the centre of Eastport, leaving behind him the semi-rural area in which he had built his home. Soon he entered an area of new brick and soaring glass, where supermarkets adjoined and a bowling alley was in its final stages of construction; then, in the older part of the town, he passed through the recognized shopping centre, crossed the traffic lights at the southern end of the market place, turned left, and entered Boyne Street, which he followed through most of its length to the Police Station. Logan was waiting for him at the edge of the curb. The chief inspector stopped beside the sergeant, glared out of the window, and said: 'Get in. You're making the street look untidy.'

Straight-faced, Logan passed round the car, opened the passenger door, and got in beside his superior. He leaned back in his seat and stretched his legs as far forward as possible to get comfortable. 'Nice afternoon, sir,' he said, his cleft chin perfectly shaved and the skin over his handsome features positively glowing with health.

'Are you taking the mickey?' Blessingay asked severely.

'You know I wouldn't do a thing like that!' the sergeant protested.

'Wouldn't you!' the chief inspector snorted, letting in the clutch with a thump and jumping the car into motion again. 'Oh, well, you've got it coming to you. Unfortunately for the Force, you've got the stuff that makes for senior rank. I'll probably end up saying: 'Yes, sir. No, sir. Three bags full, sir,' to you before I retire. But that evil day has not yet arrived. So let's get on with our work, Sergeant.'

They passed out of the lower end of Boyne Street, swung left to arc round the market place, then turned on to a road that led towards the sea front. Making another left turn near its end, they entered a large and very precisely fenced piece of ground at the approaches to Eastport Sporting Club.

'Word came in after you rang off, sir,' Logan said, as the chief inspector drove carefully between lanes of parked cars and added frequent warnings to somnambulistic pedestrians on his very French sounding horn. 'There'll be a uniformed chap to meet us at the main entrance to the Sporting Club. A constable by the name of Fuller.'

'Let's see,' Blessingay pondered. 'That's

the big bloke who looks like the Grand Duke Ferdinand or somebody, isn't it?'

'It's a way of describing him,' Logan admitted.

'Has he got something for us?'

'I believe so, sir, though the Information Room didn't say what.'

'They're a lot. I wonder why they get up in the mornings sometimes. Leave it to the men on the spot. Sounds good, doesn't it? Brer Rabbit had it worked out long ago.'

'He lasted longer than most hooks, sir,' Logan chuckled.

'Benefit of author,' Blessingay remarked, bringing the Citroen to a lurching halt near the Sporting Club's main gate. 'We don't have any.' He switched off the engine, and opened the door beside him. 'Hop out.' And a moment or two later, they walked towards a nearby wooden kiosk, beside which a massive constable wearing a moustache had appeared. The man came to attention and saluted. Blessingay nodded. 'Fuller, isn't it?'

'Yes, sir.'

'What have you got?'

The constable hesitated. He glanced over his shoulder to where a thin, balding man, with stooped shoulders and tight vinegary features, was standing. 'I think I ought to introduce this gentleman, sir,' he said, as if more impressed by the unprepossessing individual behind him than the chief inspector's question. 'Mr. Allenby-Newton, sir, the manager of the Sporting Club.'

'I know Mr. Allenby-Newton,' Blessingay said, nodding curtly as the manager stepped forward and began to speak. 'But,' he went on, deliberately cutting across Allenby-Newton's words, 'I asked you what you've got, Fuller, and I expect to be answered.'

'Sorry, sir,' the constable said, his splendid moustache twitching as he dipped into a breastpocket of his uniform after his notebook. 'I've got the number of the van used by those two phonies who said they were from the Gas Board, sir.'

Blessingay grunted and took the notebook. He looked at the page which had been opened for him. 'Two phonies.

We know for sure they were phonies?'

'We can't be dead certain, sir,' Fuller said uncomfortably. 'When Mr. Allenby-Newton rang up a Gas Board official, he was told none of their men had work to do this afternoon.'

Blessingay nodded. 'You saw the pair who did the digging?'

'I spoke to them, sir.'

'Did you, by jove!' The chief inspector squinted at the open notebook again. 'B.P.W. 1080 E. You're sure it was a Gas Board vehicle they used?'

'That's been confirmed, sir. I got a good look at it myself.'

'Where was it standing?'

The officer pointed towards the shrubbery that thrust its evergreen foliage above a fence away to the left. 'In the cul-de-sac behind the shrubbery, sir, and only a short distance from where they were working.'

'I've got the picture.' Blessingay handed the notebook back to its owner. 'You say you spoke to these men. Why? Were you suspicious?'

'Curious, sir. You don't often see Gas

Board men at work on a Saturday afternoon.'

'What made you take the number of the van?'

Fuller cleared his throat. 'I didn't do that while it was standing in the cul-de-sac, sir. I suppose you might say I got a bit of a buzz before I left those two. The fair-haired chap who was doing the digging seemed a bit agitated. He said he was in a great hurry to get on and get done. Something about his wife and kid. It sounded all right, but it didn't sit with him somehow.

'Being nothing I could put my finger on, sir, I went back to my beat, and would have forgotten about the whole business if I hadn't seen the van passing along Winslow Avenue only a short time later. The fair-haired chap and his mate looked a bit sick when they saw me again, but all sorts of reasonable explanations of why they might have left their work occurred to me, so I decided to jot down the van's number as a matter of routine. My beat took me past the cul-de-sac shortly afterwards, sir, and it was then that I saw

Mr. Allenby-Newton and the stewards bending over the trench and looking at the cut cable.'

'Precisely,' Allenby-Newton put in briskly.

Blessingay turned a cold eye on the man, then gave his full attention to Fuller again. 'What did the Gas Board phonies look like? Give me a full description of the fair-haired man, Fuller.'

'Long fair hair, sir, and a feeble moustache.' The constable stroked his own perfect growth in evident self-satisfaction. 'Scruffy, but not bad looking in a sharp featured sort of way. I had him down as a bit of a yobbo. He wasn't tall, but he had a good chest and plenty of muscle. A real rough handful, I'd say.'

'Not bad,' Blessingay approved. 'Now the other chap.'

'Shortish, fat, middle-aged, and no beauty. A bit nondescript, you might say, sir. As a matter of fact, I didn't really speak to him at all.'

'You'd recognize them both again?'

'The fair-haired chap I would, sir, but I'm not too certain about the other one.'

Blessingay nodded. 'Anything else to tell me?'

'Only that they left their work-shelter behind, sir.'

'Dabs,' the chief inspector wondered, shaking his head doubtfully to himself. 'Probably not. A thing like that would be smothered by every Tom, Dick, and Harry's. But we'll have to see. All right, Fuller, you've done pretty well. You can go back to your beat now.'

'Thank you, sir.' The constable saluted again, but he looked disappointed at being dismissed from the centre of things as he strode away and brought discipline by his very presence to a pack of leather-jacketed hooligans who were just beginning to jostle the racegoers and make a nuisance of themselves.

'Now,' Blessingay said, switching his gaze from the big officer's back to the manager of the Sporting Club. 'I apologize for putting you off Mr. Allenby-Newton, but it has to be one thing at a time.'

'I am aware of that, Chief Inspector,' the manager said stiffly. 'We, the stewards

41

and myself, want to get to the bottom of this business as much as you do.'

'And your interest is less — academic?' Blessingay asked insidiously.

'We carry a lot of responsibility, Chief Inspector,' Allenby-Newton retorted. 'The National Sporting League — the bookies, you know — will flay us alive if they have to pay out a single penny on a race that was rigged.'

'The poor old bookies,' Blessingay agreed lugubriously, turning on Sergeant Logan with a covert wink. 'B.P.W. 1080 E. I want you to get in touch with the person on the Gas Board responsible for the transport. Find out who drives the van with that number. Name, address, family facts, age, interests; the usual stuff. Get going.'

Logan inclined his head, and strode away. For a moment Blessingay watched the sergeant's tall figure threading through the crowd that was still moving towards the Sporting Club's main entrance. Then he looked Allenby-Newton in the eye again, and said: 'At what time did the telephones go dead?'

'Almost exactly on ten minutes to two. I might add that the London and Provincial Sporting News Agency people were already getting restive when it happened.'

'Restive?'

'A bad word, perhaps. The 2.15 race was no more than a card filler. Undistinguished horses and jockeys don't usually interest the average punter. The results of the races in which they take part are so unpredictable. But cumulatively speaking, bookies can lose a lot of money on long odds betting which the Chinese Laundry system is slow to assimilate. The system protects them against approximate certainties, but not against the inroads of pure chance. In the present case, Merry Morn, a known dawdler, didn't deserve the attention it was getting around a quarter to two this afternoon. There had to be something wrong. And when all the lines went dead, naturally everybody shouted Francasal.'

'I understand you've discovered a second Hatherly horse.'

'We have,' Allenby-Newton agreed.

'The mount is a quite useful filly known as Sister Sue. Apart from a white-patched fetlock, she would pass for Merry Morn anywhere. We found a tin of brown dye that had been thrown away near the transporter that brought the second horse to the course. My colleagues and I have no doubt Sister Sue was substituted for Merry Morn after the fetlock in question had been dyed. Mr. Rikeman Trunch is of the same opinion. And he ought to know his own horses.'

'I'd like to see the horse that ran in the 2.15,' the chief inspector said.

'If you'll come this way,' Allenby-Newton said, conducting Blessingay through the main gate and then leading him to an area at the rear of the Sporting Club which was covered by horse transporters.

'Have you tested for dope?' the chief inspector asked, as they approached a large cream-coloured vehicle that stood beneath some oak trees on the far side of the gathering.

'We've taken samples,' the manager replied. 'The analysis will take time, of course, but I don't think we shall find anything of that sort.'

'Probably not,' Blessingay said, tapping a finger on the cream-coloured transporter as they stopped near its lowered ramp. 'This is the one?'

'Yes,' Allenby-Newton answered, nodding an uneasy kind of greeting to the pygmy figures dressed in twill breeches and check shirts who appeared from the other side of the vehicle.

'These men are employees of the Hatherly Stables?' Blessingay asked.

'They are my employees,' snapped an athletic six-footer who strode into view around the tiny men, his aquiline features dark with rage and his hands thrust deep into the pockets of a Harris Tweed hacking coat.

'You must be Mr. Rikeman Trunch,' Blessingay observed, bristling to the atmosphere which the other exuded.

'I am Rikeman Trunch,' came the rather arrogant rejoinder.

'Detective Chief Inspector Blessingay of the Eastport C.I.D.,' Allenby-Newton introduced hastily.

'I see,' Rikeman Trunch said stiffly. 'The police.'

'In the circumstances — ' Allenby-Newton began apologetically.

'I hope you've set him straight,' Rikeman Trunch cut in.

'Now what do you mean by that, sir?' Blessingay asked quietly.

'This looks bad for me,' the trainer said bluntly.

'It doesn't look good,' Blessingay admitted.

'I had nothing to do with it. Do you hear?'

'Mr. Rikeman Trunch,' the chief inspector said shortly, 'you may play the autocrat among your own, but if anybody is going to ride the high horse here, it will be me.'

'I'd advise you to be careful, Chief Inspector,' the trainer warned. 'I'm entirely innocent of any plan to cheat or defraud. I will not be taken to task by you people, by God!'

Blessingay recalled the Deputy Chief Constable's request for use of the soft-pedal, and choked back a really nasty retort. 'Sir,' he said quietly, 'I have no intention of making a nuisance of myself or of trespassing on your rights as an individual; but I must be the best judge of my own duty. In a matter like this, you have to be guilty of something — even if it's only negligence.'

'I'm not trying to shrug off any responsibility that is rightly mine,' Rikeman Trunch retorted. 'But responsibility and blame needn't go together.'

'Then where do you place the blame?'

'On members of my staff whom I thought I could trust.'

'Be more explicit, please.'

'A month ago, I took on a new head boy named Joe Reith. He had excellent references, and up to today had given me good service. He had the entire handling of the Eastport outing. The loading of our mounts was his direct responsibility. Heavens alive, Chief Inspector! Besides the simple trust between master and man, it's what I pay for, isn't it? The villain must have been working for a gang of professional backers all along. I'll put a whip to his back when I get the chance!'

'Where is he now?' Blessingay asked.

'He's gone,' Rikeman Trunch replied. 'He's done a bunk with his pal Geordie Gedge, my second boy.'

'Can you describe them to me?'

Trunch pursed his lips, then lifted his shoulders and let them fall again. 'A pair of little fellows. Four feet ten or eleven and perhaps seven stone. Reith was wearing riding breeches and a yellow silk shirt, which was open at the neck, and Gedge was wearing a green check jacket, a red neckcloth, and cords.'

'I'll put out a call for them,' Blessingay said, glancing towards the main stand, from which a roar that sounded less than friendly had just gone up. 'What's that?'

'I've no idea,' Allenby-Newton said, looking every bit as puzzled as he sounded. 'What do you make of it, Mr. Rikeman Trunch?'

'Not a damned thing,' came the almost rude reply. 'Who knows what ails the public?' The trainer folded his arms and frowned at somebody he saw approaching. 'Who's this? One of your underlings, Chief Inspector?'

Blessingay glanced over his shoulder. He saw Logan approaching at a healthy but undignified jog-trot. 'It's my sergeant,' he said, waiting for Logan to reach them before he spoke again. 'You've been quick. Did you get what I asked for?'

'All in my notebook, sir,' the sergeant replied, panting slightly. 'I was lucky, and got on to the right man almost straight away. One of the crowd control constables said I'd find you over this way.'

Another throaty roar went up from the racecourse crowd, the sound trailing ominously into heavy echoes.

'What the devil is wrong over there?' the chief inspector demanded, gazing towards the stand. 'Do you know, Logan?'

'Not exactly, sir,' the sergeant answered. 'The constable who told me where to find you said there was some muttering in the crowd because winnings from the 2.15 race have been withheld. He thought somebody was stirring it up.'

'Very likely,' Blessingay said, his eyes narrowing. 'We can do without that.'

'It might be a good idea to radio the Station for some extra help,' Logan suggested.

'It might,' the chief inspector commented. 'But you let the uniform branch do its own work. I want to have a look at a horse.'

'Sister Sue?' Rikeman Trunch inquired.

'That's right.'

The trainer walked up the transporter's ramp, crossed the layer of straw on the floor of an outer compartment and opened a sliding door which gave access to an inner. 'In here,' he said.

'You can come, Logan,' Blessingay said, moving towards Rikeman Trunch.

They passed through the sliding door after the trainer. In the compartment beyond they came upon a sleek chestnut filly, with a soft eye and long legs. The animal shifted nervously, but calmed at once as Rikeman Trunch made a gentle clucking noise with his tongue and stroked its neck. 'Good looking girl, isn't she?' he observed with enthusiasm. 'See down there, the forelegs? The right fetlock.' He knelt, and brushed the hair covering the bony structure so that the light from the ventilation grille revealed traces of a rather glutinous substance lying upon the hide. 'See that? Dye. Cheap leather dye.' He straightened up and, twisting round, took a small tin stained by a similar substance from a nearby shelf. 'We found this in the grass outside. It needs no fancy analysis to show that this muck has been used to blot out the white streak on the filly's leg.'

'No doubt about it.' Blessingay admitted. 'Oh, take that tin, Logan. It's evidence. Thank you, Mr. Rikeman Trunch.'

The trainer handed the tin over willingly enough. 'What next?' he asked.

'I can't think of anything now,' Blessingay answered, turning out of the compartment and moving across the straw to the ramp, over which he descended rather cautiously to the ground with Logan and Rikeman Trunch following him. 'But I expect we'll be back,' he added, smiling briefly at the hovering Allenby-Newton and the stable-hands in the background. 'Come on, Logan.'

They walked away from the horse transporter and skirted the other vehicles parked in the area. 'Now what about the Gas Board man?' Blessingay asked suddenly.

Logan touched but didn't bother to consult his notebook. 'Name of Watts, sir. He's been with the Gas Board since before the dodo turned up its toes. His family has grown up, and he's a grandfather several times over. Likes his drink, but he's not a rash spender — or so his superior seems to think. He certainly doesn't fit the description of either of the men that Constable Fuller saw. He lives at number seven Chapel Street, which is in the shadow of the Gasworks. A blameless enough type, I would think.'

'We'll decide that after we've been to his house and had a talk with him.'

'Is that where we're going next, sir?'

'Yes. And I've got to call the Information Room. I want the county patrols to be on the look-out for a pair of jockey-sized rogues named Reith and

Gedge. They appear to be at the bottom of this horse substitution affair. What do you think about it all, Sergeant?'

'I don't get it, sir,' Logan answered frankly. 'It's no good trying to pretend I do. Of course, the Francasal case was long before my time, but I don't see what anybody would have to gain by repeating it today. A twice told tale — '

'Precisely, mon ami,' Blessingay agreed. 'That's what's been niggling away at my grey matter. We know that a high percentage of crooks are fools. They have to be or they wouldn't be crooks. But men with minds big enough to think in terms of the present operation — Just listen to the rumpus going on in front of the main stand!'

'It's not British,' Logan commented.

'I'm damned if it is!' the chief inspector seconded. 'It makes you ashamed!'

At this point they passed out of the Sporting Club's gate and reached the Citroen again. Blessingay opened the driver's door then, with one foot placed inside it and an elbow resting on the roof, he reverted once more to the crime they were investigating. 'This duplication just doesn't ring true. It's artificial; it lacks the saving grace of logic. It had no hope of success. I can't help wondering if it's a diversion.'

Logan looked startled. 'A diversion, sir?'

'Consider the facts.'

'Well, yes. But what would it be diverting us from?'

'Heaven knows! Your guess, Sergeant, is at least as good as mine.' Blessingay finished getting into the car, and shut the door after him.

3

Slowly and carefully, McNally backed the square and ancient Austin into the gap between buildings which opened off Cromby Lane. Then he stopped the car, and set the handbrake, but left the engine ticking over. He glanced at his wristwatch; the luminous dial showed three minutes to four; then he turned to his companion, a thick-set, blocky man, with a blue and protruding jaw, grey, expressionless eyes, bushy brows, and close-cropped black hair which was beginning to lose its colour. 'It's nearly four o'clock,' McNally said. 'We're in luck, Mr. Westmayne. There's not a soul moving in this godforsaken corner of the town.'

'Isn't that why we chose it?' Westmayne asked, slipping a woman's nylon stocking from his pocket. 'All the buildings on this lane have been condemned. Have you got your mask ready?'

McNally knocked on the glove compartment, and nodded. 'It should be any minute now.'

'I hope to goodness Fred Golson gives the signal in time. He's too fat. He's not as alert and spry as he used to be. It's the beer he keeps knocking back.'

'Fred is quids,' McNally defended. 'I'll cut out of this hiding place diagonally and ram the wall on the far side of the entrance to the pub yard. The Armoured Securities Express Car will have no choice but to swing into the opening. Pity the old Swan has been closed for a couple of years.' McNally licked his lips.

'Dave, you're as bad as Golson,' Westmayne said disgustedly. 'You're a pair of boozers.'

'We all have our little vices,' McNally said easily, turning up his watch-face again. 'This is all I seem to be doing today.'

'What?'

'Looking at the time. We're going to look a right lot of mugs, after all the trouble we've gone to planning this job, if there's a change in the armoured car's itinerary.'

'There'll be no change,' Westmayne promised stonily. 'We can do without your brand of negative thinking.'

'Sorry I spoke, Mr. Westmayne,' McNally said, inwardly smiling a very unpleasant smile. The boss was getting rattled. Westmayne's nerves weren't so good. He ought to get his imagination under control and stop spending so many nights in his housekeeper's bed. Westmayne had been good once, but now he ought to stick to his fun fair. The plain truth was that he was dated. His image of himself was that of an oldtime Chicago gangster. These days you had to squeeze two minute's work out of every minute spent. The boss no longer had it. But perhaps tomorrow he wouldn't think himself so tough and clever.

'For what length of time will one of those flame-throwers throw out a flame?' Westmayne asked.

McNally yawned his angry thoughts away. 'Plenty long enough to steam the Express people out of their shell,' he replied. 'The cylinders are full of oil, and Bill Piper and Ritchie Fairclough know exactly how to use the nozzles.'

'I don't want any slip-ups,' Westmayne warned, opening the welt of his nylon stocking and gathering in the leg with noticeably agitated fingers.

'Do any of us?' McNally asked dryly. 'I wonder if the Maharajah of Lahkpore is insured? Wouldn't it be a caution if we did the old boy a bit of good by swiping his State Jewels?'

'Your sense of humour!' Westmayne exclaimed in acidulous tones, pulling the stocking over his head and squashing his features into a shapeless blur behind the clinging nylon.

McNally shrugged in apparent tolerance. 'At least we can agree that Sir Jefferson Jepp's idea of holding an India Week at the Town Hall was the inspiration of the year. Nothing else could have brought the maharajah's jewels to lowly Eastport. The Raj is dead, but the friendship of the Old Queen's India lives on. Isn't that right, Mr. Westmayne?'

'Look, McNally,' Westmayne snapped, his voice slightly muffled. 'You're a damned sight too smart for your own good.'

'All the advantages of a State supplied Secondary Mod. education,' McNally elaborated ironically.

'Everybody is getting fed up with you.'

'I could weep for them.'

'Put your mask on. It's nearly time.'

McNally reached into the glove compartment. He took out a black nylon stocking, and waved it in the air. A faint scent of jasmine came from it.

'Gilda's?' Westmayne asked sharply.

'Gilda's,' McNally agreed, working the welt of the stocking down on to his neck. 'I'll bet it looked better on her.'

Westmayne's fist doubled and opened again. He didn't answer. Then, from inside his jacket, he took out a Mauser pistol and noisily released its safety catch.

'You won't need that!' McNally snapped.

'All you have to do,' Westmayne retorted, 'is keep your eye on the spot where Fred Golson is standing.'

'I can see Fred clearly enough. You won't need that. We don't need guns. Sandbags will do all that we have to do.'

'You're telling me, aren't you, McNally? You're actually telling me.'

It was McNally's turn to be silent.

'Don't!' Westmayne rapped.

McNally pulled at his mask to give his nose and mouth more freedom. 'It's five past four,' he said. 'If they're coming, it's time.'

'They'll come!'

McNally counted off thirty seconds. The voice in his brain began to drag the count. He felt a nervous constriction in his throat, and sweat began to prickle under the nylon. 'Hadn't you better get out?' he asked. 'I'll probably hit the wall hard, but I've got the wheel to hang on to.'

'I'm all right where I am,' Westmayne answered peevishly, dropping the automatic into his lap. 'There's almost certain to be a van full of guards running with the armoured car. That's what my gun is about. I need it to scare them.'

'That makes sense,' McNally admitted, his tone as doubtful as it was grudging. 'I hope they scare.'

'They're just ordinary men doing a job.'

Another five minutes went by. The

tension in the Austin became so acute that McNally's flesh squirmed against its covering cloth.

'God, they're late!' Westmayne suddenly exploded, a hand clawing at his throat.

'Yes,' McNally agreed, his voice infuriatingly calm for all his own symptoms. 'Perhaps the blue-boys have fluffed what the trouble we made for them at the racecourse was all about.'

'That's impossible!' Westmayne almost shrieked. 'Shut up! Just shut up! This run by the Armoured Securities Express is a secret, even from the Police. Bribing that man in A.S.E. office has already cost me ten thousand pounds.'

'Cost us,' McNally corrected, first softly whistling and then beginning to sing the words of an old trumpet march. 'One more mile to go, just one more mile to go. One more mile, just one more mile — one more mile to go.' He stopped abruptly, and turned his wrist over again. 'Seven minutes overdue.' Sighing, he gazed through the windscreen and the conjoining shadows on either side of the opening before him. He saw Fred Golson leaning against a corner of the wall at the entrance to the pub yard. The man was smoking and looking, oh, so bored. Fred was probably having his doubts, too. Every man to his dream. To drown in best bitter was one, and to see Gilda rising like Venus from the waves at Cannes was another. McNally shivered pleasurably over his dream. He just had to make it come true. He must taste the sweet life while he was still young enough to enjoy it. Much as he would like to see Westmayne's pride take a tumble, the job had to be on. Where in hell was that armoured car? Where?

Then Fred Golson straightened up, and stepped back into the opening. He took the cigarette from his mouth and held it vertically at the level of his nose. McNally realized that the signal had been given. His left hand snapped the vehicle into gear and, releasing the handbrake, he let in the clutch and accelerated across the lane. A second later, he smashed into the wall on the right of the entrance to the pub yard. The impact flung him over the wheel and drove his crown against the roof. He dropped back into his seat more than a little dazed, but he had the presence of mind to thrust open the door beside him and jump into the road. On the other side Westmayne did the same. At that moment a skidding Dormobile crashed into the back of the Austin and drove it almost squarely across the lane. No vehicle bigger than a motorcycle could possibly find room to pass the old car now.

McNally dipped a hand into his trouser pocket. He drew out a sandbag. Blinking dazedly, he saw three men in maroon battle-suits and crash helmets come scrambling out of the Dormobile. Then he glimpsed the rapid approach of a large vehicle with armoured sides and the hint of a turret on top. As had been planned, the driver of the armoured car, coming in at speed from a corner, was so taken by surprise by the presence of the road-block, that he braked violently and took the only evasive action open to him. Burning rubber, he slewed into the pub yard and skidded to a standstill. Meantime, the three guards from the Dormobile had raised their enormous clubs and were looking for trouble. McNally saw one of them rushing at him. The man was a daunting sight: a natural giant of six feet six and nineteen stones; but McNally went in under the other's swinging bludgeon, thumped a fist into the man's stomach and, as he doubled up, brought the sandbag down across the giant's nape with all his force. The guard slumped into insensibility.

Staggering forward, McNally passed round the back of the locked vehicles and made for the other two guards, who were converging on a white-faced and badly shaken Westmayne. But one of the men, either seeing or hearing his approach, rounded on him and struck out aggressively. Dodging again, McNally tugged the stocking off his head and spat in the guard's face; and, as the man jerked back in surprise, spun sideways and dug an elbow into his solar plexus. The guard doubled up, crying out in pain, but a knee in the mouth silenced him, and he, too, toppled on to his face.

Turning, McNally peered anxiously to find out what was happening between Westmayne and the third guard. He saw that the Express man had driven the gang boss into a corner. Westmayne had his pistol thrust out before him, and kept repeating the warning that he would shoot. But the guard seemed to have no fear of the threat. He closed in with club uplifted for a stunning blow. McNally dived after the man, but was too late to prevent the tragedy. Westmayne fired. The guard jerked round and, with his jaw dropped and his thick arms groping, he weaved ponderously towards the Austin; but before he could reach its support, the Mauser exploded a second time. After that a number of bullets followed and, as the echo of the shots rolled between the walls on either side of the lane, the guard flopped down with two or three rivulets of blood zigzagging away from him through the dust.

'You mad-brained idiot!' McNally stormed at his boss. 'I ought to brain you!'

'Don't you touch me!' Westmayne

roared hysterically. 'I'll give you the same!'

'Murderer!' McNally taunted bitterly, grinding round on his heel and running into the pub yard.

He heard the roaring of flame-throwers immediately, and stopped at the inner corner of the building. Throwing up an arm to protect his face from the heat and glare, he moved towards the two men who were playing tongues of scarlet and orange fire on the armoured car. The reek of melting paint was already strong in the air, and McNally saw it running down the soot-encrusted sides of the vehicle. Tortured movements showed in the interior of the car. The beleaguered guards inside must already be suffering terribly from the heat. In another minute the armoured walls of the machine would be red hot. The occupants had reached their moment of decision. They must either open the rear doors and jump out or literally fry in their own fat.

The seconds ticked away. Still there was no sign of the guards abandoning their vehicle. McNally kicked a heel against the ground to ease his frustration. Surely the fools weren't going to be faithful until death? Before long, some member of the public, alerted by the shots from Westmayne's gun, would appear on the scene. That might very well mean another killing. McNally didn't want anybody else to die. 'The bloody fools!' he yelled at Golson, who was crouched toad-like a few yards to his right.

Then the back doors of the armoured car burst open. They clanged back against the metal sides, and soot and flaked cellulose fluttered from them. The occupants, three men again, their faces scarlet and the hair almost scorched from the exposed parts of their bodies, jumped into the yard and began to beat at their smoking clothing. They stumbled aimlessly away from the heat, all the fight gone out of them, and McNally and Golson struck them down without meeting the slightest resistance.

The flame-throwers turned aside and spluttered out. McNally ran to the rear of the armoured car. He jumped inside it.

The stifling heat pressed about him like that of an oven. He heard the metal walls singing as they began to contract. Clawing his collar open and gasping for breath, he peered about him, the effort bringing excess moisture into his eyes. He saw a wooden chest lying on the floor between the seats that ran along the sides of the car. He tugged at the inch thick lid, half expecting to find it locked, but it opened easily enough, and inside the chest he saw a large silver casket. The lid of this container did prove to be locked, but as he was certain that he had found the jewels of Lahkpore, he raised the casket against his chest and turned and jumped out into the yard, where hands instantly reached out to relieve him of his burden. 'I'll carry it,' he said, nodding to Westmayne, who was standing in the entrance to the yard, gun still out and his face grey and exposed again.

'Let's go!' the gang boss ordered hoarsely. 'You all know what to do!'

Not a word was spoken or a gesture made. The gang broke up and fled from the yard. Their footfalls set up a high-pitched metallic ringing against the walls. Moving to the left, they rounded the road-block and followed the lane for about fifty yards. Then McNally and Westmayne broke away from their three companions and turned into an alley on the right. Golson, Piper, and Fairclough turned into a similar alley on the other side of the lane and disappeared.

Westmayne led the way along the narrow, heat-choked passage. He set up a good pace, but McNally managed to ignore the weight of the casket and keep up with him. Cracking walls leaned above them, the pitted underfoot caught at their toes, and a hundred tiny windows, blanked out by grey dust and cobwebs, peered at them like the eyes of the dead. A furtive mongrel jumped out of a recess, and snarled. McNally kicked out at the brute, almost dropping the casket in the process, and stumbled for some distance before fully regaining both his hold and his stride. The air was burning in his lungs, and the blood pounding in his temples. He was tiring fast, but fortunately there wasn't much farther to go.

Halting at the beginning of a curve in the alley, Westmayne threw an anxious glance behind him; then, relief passing across his suddenly mobile face, he shouldered open a big gate on the right and entered a large and dusty yard. McNally followed him across the enclosure and up to the wall of another large and long-abandoned building. Here Westmayne opened a door and they continued their progress along a debris-littered passage, which was partially blocked at its end by a door that canted on twisted hinges. The door shrilled and ground as the gang boss forced it open. Then they moved into a garage, where the gauzy work of spiders and time's erosion had covered the splintered benches and rusty tools in a winding sheet through which only sombre outlines were visible. The one dustfree object in the room was a Ford ten hundredweight van. This stood opposite a pair of battered double-doors, which let in a dozen darts and splurges of mote-laden sunshine. Westmayne opened the rear doors of the van. McNally dumped the casket on the floor of the

70

vehicle, and pulled a number of large pulp sacks over it. Westmayne shut the doors again, and quickly locked the handle; then he ran and got in behind the wheel, while McNally drew the bolts at the entrance. They paused a moment and pulled the stocking masks off their sweating faces and stuffed them into their pockets. Then McNally forced open the double-doors, and the gang boss drove the van out of the garage and turned left into the lane beyond it. After shutting up behind them, McNally ran to where the van was waiting for him, got in beside Westmayne, and made a sign to get going.

For fifty yards they followed the lane, then Westmayne eased the van round a sharp corner and they passed into a continuation of the alley along which they had made their getaway from the scene of the robbery. The gang boss drove slowly between the closely confining walls, and sighed with relief as the vehicle nosed clear of the built-up area and turned on to the road which ran parallel with the river.

Westmayne drove towards the sea,

picking up speed for a while, but slowing again through an area where the concrete road had sunk behind the great piles that helped defend the banks from the lift of the tides. McNally gazed across the river's turgid flow. The scene ahead and to the south conveyed an impressionistic effect of ships and jibs and arching warehouses. Mist and bending sunbeams had made a mockery of perspective and geometric progressions. Colours blurred into shadows, and shadows blurred back into colour. The river's most distant points of sullen opacity threw up a dancing refulgence in which the slicing wings of half-seen birds cut prismatic arcs. Above the rooftops that flanked the dimly converging banks, the sky rolled back from storm yellow to beaten gold then fell seawards in a line of fire-brick haze that held the smudged patterns of the larger buildings of the town.

The van hit a pothole and lurched. Westmayne swore. McNally took his eyes off the scenery and looked at his boss. Westmayne had the appearance of a squeezed-out orange; he was still sweating and shaking uncontrollably. For a moment McNally wondered if conscience were troubling the man: murder was a crime to shake the most callous; but then he realized that Westmayne's condition amounted to the further development of his earlier diagnosis. Westmayne could no longer live with the realities of crime. The pressures were too much for him. He was a menace to himself and everybody else. One of these times he was going to crack up completely. McNally grimly assured himself that he wasn't going to be around when that happened. He took his eyes off Westmayne as a wave of repugnance passed through him. Aside from the matter of the murder, his personal antipathy was so strong that he wanted to stop the van and jump out. Anything to get away from Westmayne's company!

The gang boss looked round. His face darkened; he seemed to have caught at least the atmosphere of McNally's thoughts; but he said: 'I'm sorry, Dave; I had to do it. That guard would have smashed my head in.'

'I was right behind him,' McNally

retorted, his voice so harsh that he hardly recognized it. 'You didn't have to pull the trigger.'

'A split second counts in a tight corner,' Westmayne pleaded.

'Murder is still murder,' McNally snapped. 'The coppers will hound us now.'

'They would have hounded us anyway.'

'You had thoughts of turning the Mauser on me.'

'You had thoughts of hitting me.'

'If this job starts coming to bits — ' McNally muttered through tight jaws, his head shaking slowly.

'It won't!' Westmayne's mouth gave a vicious twist. He swung the van away from the quay and on to a road that led towards the centre of the town. 'What's up with you, Dave?'

'I don't like murder.'

'I suppose you think you're incapable of it,' Westmayne sneered, slowing at an intersection then juggling with the gears as he moved out into the fairly heavy traffic passing through a main thorough-fare. 'You're not incapable of it, Dave. In the right circumstances, every man is capable of it. Just pray that fate or whatever it is doesn't find your weak spot.'

'I'm not a nut case.'

'Neither am I. Without me, those jewels wouldn't be lying in the back of the van.'

'That doesn't prove much.'

'Dave, you're a bad-tempered, bigoted, unforgiving so-and-so. We've got what we set out to get. Nobody said it would be easy, and it hasn't been. You get nothing in this world without suffering a bit and taking a few risks.'

'On plush?'

'Oh, that's some of it, is it?' Westmayne commented bitterly. 'I've had by far and away the worst of it. Ever tried to deal with greedy little blighters like those racing boys, Reith and Gedge? They'd skin a herring bone. I had to persuade them to work for us without telling them damn all that mattered. Have you got any idea what a hell of a long and exhausting job it was to set up the phone calls for those late bets on that bloody horse? Man, you're the one who's been on — !'

The violent clangour of a police bell sounded from along the street. Westmayne's face went ashen again. He tightened up so badly at the wheel that he had to brake sharply to avoid running into the car ahead. Then he brought his chin a couple of painful inches to the right and watched a black patrol car go flashing by on the opposite side of the street. His Adam's apple bobbed as he swallowed hard, and he almost made another mistake at the approaches to a busy zebra crossing. 'Looks like the ball has opened,' he said with an attempt at jocularity as he jolted to a stop. 'I think we've fixed for the coppers to be at sixes and sevens while the boys lay our false trail.'

'Good show!' McNally minced in a provoking imitation of his companion's educated accents. 'You're going to have to watch those nerves, Mr. Westmayne.'

'And you,' Westmayne gritted, moving across the zebra strip, 'are going to have to watch your tongue. I've put up with enough.'

'Sooner or later,' McNally persisted, 'a

nervous man makes a big mistake.'

'I made my biggest mistake,' came the biting retort, 'when I brought you into my operations.'

McNally smiled to himself. He was content to let his boss have the last word. After all, who wished to argue with the truth?

4

Pipe in mouth and head thrust out before him, Blessingay strode away from the damp-encrusted terrace home of Ernie Watts, the Gas Board man. He made for the Citroen, which was parked in a wider and more accessible area near the entrance to Chapel Street. Nearing the car, he slowed to let Sergeant Logan, who had been extending reassurances to the anxious Mrs. Watts, catch up with him. As the sergeant came up to his elbow, he slanted a rather savage grimace and said: 'Our Ernie, eh? Half-slewed?'

'Pie-eyed, sir,' Logan agreed. 'He must have had enough to float a canoe before they stopped serving at half past two. His condition rules out his having played any sort of active part in the racecourse affair.'

'Indeed and indeed,' Blessingay concurred. 'I suppose he was rational?'

'Just about with it, sir. But not much

help to anybody.'

'Drunk or sober,' the chief inspector observed. 'He can't even obey the Gas Board's rules. He knows he's not supposed to leave his vehicle on that piece of waste ground; but he does it all the same. The fact remains, the world and his wife seem to know what Ernie does with his van when it's not in use, and it's much too far from his house for him to hear it should it be started up. Almost anybody could have borrowed it today.'

'I'm afraid so, sir.'

Blessingay lengthened his stride as he neared the Citroen. He could hear the warning buzzer on his radio sounding. 'We'll have the dabs boys run the usual check over the van, Logan. I don't see what else we can do. Let's hope somebody manages to pick up Reith and Gedge. We need a bit of linkage.' He stopped beside the car and, opening the driver's door, reached inside and pressed the transmit switch on his radio. 'Hello, Information Room,' he said into the microphone. 'This is the Chief Inspector. Have you got something for me? Over.'

The reply came in a voice that was clinically detached and impersonal. 'A report has come in of a robbery in Cromby Lane. Masked men, armed and carrying flame-throwers, stopped an armoured car and guard van belonging to the Armoured Securities Express Company. One of the company's guards has been shot dead; others have been severely hurt. An ambulance has been despatched to the scene of the hold-up, and a patrol car is standing by. Over.'

'Thank you, Information Room,' Blessingay said. 'I will attend with Sergeant Logan. Give me the robbery's objective, please. Over.'

'Our report is incomplete and unconfirmed — '

'Tell me what was pinched,' the chief inspector cut in, jiggling at the switch in his exasperation.

'The State Jewels of Lahkpore,' the voice over the air answered disapprovingly. 'The jewels were on the way to the Town Hall for display during the forthcoming India Week. Over.'

'Why weren't we told of this — this

consignment, Information Room?' Blessingay demanded. 'Over.'

'It was supposed to be a secret. Over.'

'Some secret!' the chief inspector barked. 'Anything else? Over.'

'We have no further information,' came the reply. 'Over.'

'Thank you,' Blessingay replied. 'We're on our way to Cromby Lane. Over and out.'

A switch clicked and the channel went dead. Blessingay slipped into his seat and pulled a face at Logan, who had already got into the seat opposite. 'Well, well,' he said, as he started up and moved off. 'Now we know. I heard something about the Maharajah of Lahkpore and his confounded jewels about a month ago. His Highness will get no sympathy from me. If only we'd been told!' He chuckled rather sourly. 'Some headwork went into this one, Logan. Firstly, whoever conceived the job knew that shipping the jewels to Eastport was to be a secret. That argues top inside information. The repeat Francasal scare, the runaway stable chaps, the dye, and the rest of it; pretty good. Imagination plus organization. Why don't we get brains like that in the Force? Anyway, we swallowed the lot, have been chasing our tails, and now that we need our resources, find them scattered all over the place. I'd take my hat off to somebody if it wasn't for the killing. Ever been mugged, Logan?'

'Once or twice, sir,' the sergeant admitted dryly.

'We'll call it in,' Blessingay promised, weaving in and out of traffic as he crossed the town centre, 'twenty one shillings in the pound.'

Just then the radio buzzed, and Logan took a rather unnecessary confirmation from the head offices of Armoured Securities Express that the State Jewels of Lahkpore had indeed been stolen from one of their vehicles.

'Tacit,' Blessingay growled, turning into the condemned area of which Cromby Lane formed a part. 'Now turn it over to the professionals.'

'It always gets to us in the end,' Logan agreed.

They reached the scene of the robbery

a minute later. Blessingay stopped and they both got out. The ambulance was just pulling away. The chief inspector watched it pass from sight, then moved over to the patrol car, which had been backed into an opening on the right near the locked vehicles that formed a roadblock. Two smart-looking officers in cheese-cutters and buskins stepped forward and saluted. Neither man had yet reached thirty, but the taller of the pair had the lean, hungry, prematurely mature appearance of an ambitious man who was prepared to go to almost any lengths to better himself. The other constable was plumper and better looking, but he had placid eyes and a certain slackness about the mouth. Blessingay was not impressed. 'Names?' he demanded.

'Carter and Venables, sir,' the taller constable said.

'You're Carter?'

'Yes, sir.'

'Where's the dead man, Carter?'

'We've carried him into the yard behind the old pub, sir, and thrown a blanket over him.'

'Called the mortuary?'

'Yes, sir.'

'Shot, wasn't he?'

'It looks as if somebody emptied a gun into him, sir,' Carter replied. 'He isn't very pretty.'

'Show me.'

The constables led Blessingay and Logan into the yard at the rear of the building opposite. Blessingay saw the fire-scarred armoured car, with its gaping doors at the back, the heat-cracked glass behind its grilles, and the burned oil lying about its melted tyres. But he reserved the best of his attention for the shrouded body lying under a wall, and was careful to keep his features expressionless as Carter threw back the blanket and revealed the guard's contorted face and riddled body. 'Vicious,' he commented.

'The man who did this will be a good one to watch, sir,' Carter observed, rather daring.

The chief inspector nodded sombrely. 'We've had trigger-happy Hank's to deal with before today. We'll get him, constable. All right; that will do. Cover him up again. Did you manage to glean much from the A.S.E. guards?'

'Only what's fairly obvious, sir,' Carter answered. 'None of the guards was in any shape to talk a lot. Apparently the old Austin that's now blocking the road shot out in front of the Dormobile and caused a bit of a pile up. The armoured car anchored up and skidded in here, which is what seems to've been intended for it. There was a bit of a fight, some sandbagging, and then the gun was used. After that the armoured car was steamed open by a couple of men with flame-throwers, and the guards inside were forced out. They were sandbagged straight away. When they came round, the ambulance was here, and the jewels were gone.'

'Who gave notice of the robbery?'

'Somebody phoned the Station, sir. I believe they've got his name and address.'

'They'd better have.' Blessingay turned round and looked at Logan. 'All we've got that's likely to tell us anything is the old Austin.'

'Excuse me, sir,' Carter broke in.

Blessingay frowned. 'What?'

'I've been through to the Information Room about the Austin, sir. It was pinched from Tapwell Street in Lowestoft this morning.'

'Good man,' the chief inspector murmured.

'The point of origin?' Logan wondered.

'Probably not.'

Logan's brows lifted. 'No prophet cometh out of . . . etc?'

'Don't be daft, Logan!' Blessingay exclaimed. 'I wasn't trying to imply that only big city men can think up and carry out large scale crimes. There are as many brains, both good and bad, in Lowestoft as in anywhere else. It's simply standard procedure for hooks bent on big business to nick a car some distance away from where they intend to operate. The chance of the vehicle being recognized as stolen is that much smaller. That would be especially true where an antique model like the one out in the lane was concerned. It goes back to the early thirties; there aren't many of them left now. But I must say, I can't think of a better car than this particular Austin vintage to run into a brick wall. They're tough old girls.'

They walked out to the lane, with Blessingay slightly in the lead, and he pointed at once to the patrol car, where the radio could be heard buzzing urgently. Carter ran over to the vehicle, thrust an arm through the open window, switched on, and gave the car's code number. 'It's for you, sir,' he called to Blessingay.

The chief inspector strode over to the car, 'Go ahead, please, Information Room,' he said into the microphone.

'A report has been received,' came the reply, 'that a green Rover 2000 was seen leaving town on the Norwich road at high speed by a man with a stocking mask over his face. The car had two other occupants, similarly masked. Over.'

'Have you got the number of the Rover? Over.'

'Only part of the registration. It's believed to begin M.P. something and to include the figures 47. Over.'

'Alert Norwich and the county patrols,' Blessingay ordered. 'Sergeant Logan and

I are going to motor towards Norwich. Over and out.' Turning, he walked towards the Citroen, jerking a thumb for the sergeant to follow quickly.

They ducked into the vehicle and took their seats again. Blessingay spun the engine, reversed gingerly into the middle of the road, then arced into a cut-back of sorts. Slipping into forward gear, he spun his wheel to the left and accelerated away from the condemned area, passing out of Cromby Lane and picking up the arterial road that led to the county town some thirty miles away. 'I cut 'em short back there,' he said, as they sped by the railway station. 'I was half expecting Albert Bryant to come on the air. I hate having to account for my every thought and movement.'

'Yes, sir,' Logan murmured dutifully.

'The top brass never seem to realize that I know exactly what I'm looking for.'

'Yes, sir.'

'Do you know what I'm looking for?'

'Yes, sir.'

Blessingay quirked an amused eyebrow. 'Well?'

'An abandoned green Rover 2000. Not too many miles out of Eastport, sir. It may even be a little way up a side road.'

'Do you know, Sergeant,' the chief inspector said, deadly serious for a moment, 'it's frightening to have another man know your mind so well. Keep your eyes open.' His right heel braced, Blessingay kept the speed of his car down to about thirty-five miles an hour and, as they cruised along, he kept his own gaze drifting from left to right and back again. The country on either side of the road was flat and green and low-hedged; no object the size of a Rover 2000 could be safely hidden in the immediate vicinity; and as the side-turnings were few and by the same token exposed for long stretches at their beginnings, he let the car run on without any sort of check or pause. It wasn't until they had left Eastport six miles behind them, and were about a mile from the village of Burgh, that Blessingay noticed that the verge on the corner of a lane leading off to the right had recently been ripped by the skidding tyre of a car which had taken it too quickly.

'Classic,' Logan observed.

'We're a pair of clever chaps,' Blessingay agreed ironically and, without giving much warning to a motorist in his wake, swung off into the lane and winced as a poor surface began to rock the Citroen and hack at his tyres. They covered about two hundred yards and then the lane curved sharply to the left and began to move steeply downhill. Higher hedges now threw shadows across the way. They approached a tree-clustered hollow, where chalk glimmered through the breeze-stirred traceries on their right. Blessingay applied the brakes. A gateway appeared, and the thick dust before it showed the confused but recent impress of car tyres. Pulling off the road, the chief inspector drew to a halt and got out, gesturing that his companion should do the same. Then he took his pipe from his pocket, blew through it, and jammed it into the corner of his mouth, his teeth showing in a brief yellow gleam as they clamped upon the stem. After that he walked through the gateway and down the sloping path which led through bushes and light tree-growth into the abandoned chalk-workings below. He heard Logan descending in a checked run behind him. His nostrils twitched. The smells of dry earth, dusty leaf, and ageing herbs were faintly infiltrated by exhaust odours that clung to the heavy air near the ground; tyretracks were also very much in evidence where sand patched the approaches to the bottom of the pit. Then the arena-like space under the steep wall of the workings came into full view, and, turning, Blessingay kissed his fingertips dramatically and said: 'Voilà.'

'There she blows!' Logan agreed. 'One Rover 2000. Registration number M.P.W. 8472. The Information Room got somewhere near it.'

'But they're simply not in our class,' Blessingay said smugly. 'And what do the tyre-tracks tell you?'

'One came in, sir, and another went out.'

'Exactly.' The chief inspector started retracing his steps up the slope. 'The Rover won't run away. Will you be so good as to suggest the next move, Sergeant.'

'Certainly, sir,' Logan said, falling in with the passing light-heartedness of his superior's mood. 'We must get back into your car and drive on. I don't think we shall need to go much farther.'

'Up the hill, and down the hill,' Blessingay agreed.

They completed the climb, and re-entered the Citroen. The chief inspector touched the starter and pulled off the verge. They went up the hill that rose before them, then motored down the other side. Ahead of them they saw wide open country and the runways of Burgh Airfield, with the main hangar and its largely derelict subsidiary buildings over to the right. Blessingay followed a curve in the lane, and turned left through a gateway that gave on to a tarmac road which ended abruptly against a cracking concrete apron, where slightly raised foundations and a pile or two of rubble indicated the vanished command block from which U.S. bomber generals and their executive colonels had once directed the great daylight raids against the Third

Reich. Blessingay stopped beside one of the rubble piles and left the car again. He gazed around him, taking in the great shining emptiness under the sun, and listened to the liquid cooing of pigeons as it came in down the breeze. The birds held court; as ever, the old tent-maker's irony was fulfilled. But Blessingay shook the vagrant thought from his mind. He glanced across the top of the car at Logan and said: 'Which one shall we try first?'

'Working on the principle that clever men are often the most impatient, sir, I'd say the first shed we come to.'

'Very good, Logan. Let's walk.' And with the sergeant moving up to his elbow, the chief inspector strode away to the right, heading for a long black shed which pointed its unseen doorway to the west. They had covered half the ground between them and the building, when Blessingay said: 'Do you like Mozart, Logan?'

'Mozart, sir?' Logan sounded surprised. 'I can take him or leave him. I'm no rabid music fan in any direction.'

'Great man for solving problems, was

Mozart,' Blessingay observed. 'He had a sort of relentless quality. He would never give up on a musical idea until he had extracted everything possible from it. When you believe Mozart has done all he can do, he always surprises you by doing a bit more. Surprises of that type, Logan, are the real surprises.'

'An attribute of greatness, sir,' Logan suggested, a little patronisingly.

'No doubt,' the chief inspector agreed, frowning to himself, for he had always envied his subordinate's vastly superior education. 'I was listening to the 'Jupiter' Symphony when you horrors down at the Station dug me out of my chair and put me to work again. For me, the 'Jupiter' is the greatest symphony ever. One of these days, I'll hear it all through again.'

'Too bad about your afternoon off,' Logan said sympathetically. 'The Force is a hard master.'

Blessingay didn't appear to hear the words. 'In the last movement of the 'Jupiter',' he went on, 'Mozart appears to be covering endless ground. So he is, but it's really a kind of trick, because he never really leaves his premise. He moves all the way round it and upwards in an ever decreasing spiral. Then down he comes with a bump and ends exactly where he began.'

'Interesting, sir,' Logan said politely.

'Yes,' Blessingay countered dryly. 'But don't let it bother you. I've still got all my marbles.'

Logan cleared his throat.

They had reached the door of the black building. This appeared to save the sergeant a lot of embarrassment. He thrust his hands into a gap between the sliding doors and pushed them apart. Inside the building stood a Morris Minor. Logan strode forward and placed a hand on its bonnet. 'It's still warm,' he said, unable for a moment to hide his satisfaction.

'Well done, Sergeant,' Blessingay applauded.

'But it was pretty obvious, sir, wasn't it?' Logan said modestly. 'After making such a big haul, no gang in its right senses would stay in this country. Stands to reason, they'd get out just as fast as they could. I expect their aircraft is well on the way to the Continent by now. Shall I run back to the car and get on the radio, sir? Paris, Brussels and Amsterdam ought to be warned as soon as possible.'

'No hurry,' Blessingay soothed. 'Let's have a good look around first, shall we?'

'But where's the need, sir?' demanded the mystified Logan.

Blessingay pulled an ear. 'What's my biggest fault, Logan?'

The sergeant blew out his cheeks, and gestured hopelessly.

'An unfair question,' the chief inspector agreed. 'You can't say. I might not like it; it could be more than your job's worth. Well, I'll tell you. I've no faith in human nature. Not an atom. I don't trust anybody. I believe nothing I hear, and only half of what I see. In other words, I'm one of the most suspicious and mistrustful old devils you'd meet in a day's march.'

'You're extremely self-analytical, sir,' Logan said carefully. 'One might say self-critical.'

'Oh, I'm having one of my days,'

Blessingay admitted. 'Anyhow, it's said. Now let's go and have a look around.' He placed his hands on his hips and let his gaze pass through a slow arc as his ungainly body swivelled. Then he pointed northwards, to a spot about a mile away, where the shape of a barn was just visible among a number of small oaks. 'I think we'll go that way.'

Logan showed traces of irritability. He stepped out as if he wanted to get an irksome chore over with. But Blessingay forced him to slow down by setting a comfortable pace. He took a rather sardonic pleasure in the younger man's not so secret annoyance. Logan became rigid in his ideas the instant he made up his mind; his brain could be one track and literal at times. He needed a lesson. The present circumstances might provide one. On the other hand, if the sergeant did happen to be right, and this trek across the airfield did prove a waste of time — Well, a certain chief inspector might find an explanation difficult to come by. But Blessingay felt in his bones that he wasn't wrong. And this feeling was further encouraged when he saw a very new looking cigarette end lying crushed on the rough surface of the runway before him. He said nothing, but a sidelong glance revealed that a frowning Logan had also seen the cigarette end. Now let him start worrying a bit; it wouldn't do him any harm.

They kept moving forward. A few hundred yards further on, where the roughness of uncultivated land pressed in about the concrete strip, Blessingay saw a nylon stocking which the breeze had wrapped around a clump of tall and bending grasses. Logan's frown reappeared and showed signs of becoming permanent. Blessingay picked the stocking up, extended it, turned it over in a quick examination, then folded it up and slipped it into his pocket, all without saying a word.

'It's not unusual to see a woman's stocking lying around these days,' Logan commented. 'It could have been dropped down by the hangar and blown up here.'

'It could've,' the chief inspector agreed, wetting a finger and holding it up to ascertain the direction of the wind. 'West,' he said.

Logan glanced back to the south, and shrugged. 'People use the countryside as a litter bin these days.'

'So they do,' Blessingay admitted — 'so they do.'

They reached the end of the runway without seeing anything else that was suspicious. Leaving the concrete strip, they stepped into the long grass and made for the barn, which was now only a hundred or two yards away. They came to the oak trees and passed beneath them. Then they walked along the side of the barn and turned into the wide doorway at its opposite end. The building had a cool atmosphere and carried the smells of cows and rotting hay. Blessingay bent and, his hands resting upon his thighs, began a careful inspection of the hoofrutted floor. There was little of interest to be seen, though there were definite treadmarks near the centre of the place, where the dust was thickest. Then, just as he was beginning to fear that the difficult explanation was going to be necessary after all, Blessingay lighted upon several small but damning droplets of damp that carried traces of rust. 'A leaking radiator, would you say?' he asked gruffly. 'People really ought to drain off their anti-freeze at the end of the winter.'

'There has been a car standing here,' Logan admitted with better grace than his superior had hoped for. Then, while Blessingay stood to one side, he bent and used his younger eyes to pick out the course followed by the vehicle as it had left the barn for the road which ran across a gap in the nearby hedge. He paused on the slightly broken verge and gazed to left, nodding awkwardly as he gazed back across his shoulder.

'Back to where they started?' the chief inspector called significantly.

'It's a strong possibility, sir,' Logan conceded.

'I think it's strong enough to regard as a certainty.'

The sergeant smiled wryly, and retraced his steps towards the barn. 'Even so, the radio call would have done no harm, sir.'

Blessingay shrugged. 'Perhaps not. But

I'll bet a year's pay the men we want are back in Eastport. They've given us credit for quite a lot of sense, but they think they're just that bit smarter. This means they've probably got a deal planned with a local fence. Who'd think of that, eh? East Anglia with its reputation for being so backward in these matters. I wonder who would be big enough — or at least bold enough — to do the buying?'

'Somebody without a smell of a record,' Logan suggested. 'We may be after a bunch of stir-virgins. As you've said, sir, there's a good head at work behind this job. The real wide-boys don't get caught. Perhaps they won't this time.'

'You're a pessimist, Logan,' Blessingay said, indicating that they might as well start walking back to the Citroen. 'The cleverest of them make mistakes in the end.'

'Any idea who we're after, sir?'

'Not a clue, Sergeant,' Blessingay sighed. 'We'll keep pegging away at the routine stuff until we get a break. But I don't think it will be long in coming. This case is *too* big to stay quiet for long.'

5

McNally looked around the living room of Gilda Kemp's flat. It was a nice flat: modern and full of comfort. Gilda kept it spotless. A fastidious girl, Gilda. But then, she deserved the best and always got it. She'd even got him, hadn't she? He grinned at his own reflection in the hand-painted mirror that hung above the cocktail cabinet. He looked sharp in his new suit, with its narrowest of narrow lapels, figure-hugging lilac waistcoat, and elegant drainpipes. He was confident that he could have any girl he fancied. But he'd settle for Gilda. Gilda was every woman rolled into one. Not that she was faultless; far from it. His mouth twisted wryly, and he made a small adjustment to his tie. Her special fault was that she liked to keep him waiting. He had been in the flat ten minutes now. She ought to have finished dressing by this time. 'Hurry up!' he called towards the bedroom door.

'Have you pulled the plug on yourself, honey?'

There was no reply. He didn't expect one. Gilda seldom wasted words — except when she got angry; then look out. Ambling to the far side of the room, he took a cigarette from a silver box on a table there, struck a match, and gave himself a light. As he was exhaling, Gilda came into the room. She took very little notice of him; but that was normal too. She wore a variety of trouser suit that did her perfect figure no harm at all, and the lacquer on her corn-yellow hair caused it to glow like harvest sunshine. She also took a cigarette from the box, then moved towards him, the cigarette held between two straight fingers as she raised it towards pouting lips. He struck another match, his heart beating a little faster as he held out the flame to her. Her skin — ? There was that old simile about Dresden china. Well, that's what her skin was like: Dresden china; and her eyes, as round and long-lashed as anybody could wish, were coloured somewhere between pure violet and smoky lavender. Her nose was straight, and her chin dimpled. There was not a line in sight; her face bore no trace of age. She seemed as ageless and as timeless as beauty itself.

But there was a coldness in her. He always sensed it and tried to ignore it. Yet it wasn't coldness as most men thought of coldness. Gilda in her orgasmic moments generated enough heat to melt the poles. This coldness came from the spirit rather than the flesh. It was hard and calculating: a mockery which called the soul its own, and sold what it appeared to give. Gilda's one true love was Gilda. She would always put herself first. You couldn't trust such a woman. It was another of those things which McNally knew but wished to forget. He wasn't an idealist, yet he realized that he loved like one, and in his dark moments he wondered how it would end.

Stubbing out his cigarette in an ashtray, he moved towards the girl and gathered her into his arms. Her supple form seemed to flow and mould against his own. The feel of her flesh beneath the silk she was wearing had a galvanic effect on his libido. He smothered her face with kisses, and nibbled at her ear, while his hands passed freely over her body. Then, to his surprise, Gilda pushed him from her and slipped out of his embrace, her cigarette still held between the two straight fingers and the thickish ash upon its end seeming to emphasize her indifference. 'Hey!' he exclaimed, a little hurt. 'What's up with you?'

Gilda smiled mechanically, and gave him what passed for a fond shove. 'I've got a headache, Dave,' she said. 'You will read that damned Kama Sutra before you come here.'

'That's nice,' he said, half angrily now. 'I haven't looked inside that book for months. Who needs to anyway? Why don't you take a couple of aspirins?'

'No.'

He stiffened and held his ground, staring at her glumly. 'It's Saturday evening, honey.'

'I don't feel like it tonight,' she retorted. 'You don't own me.'

McNally felt as if he had been slapped. 'Is there somebody else?' he asked.

'And if there were?' she countered.

'Is there?' he demanded, his shoulders stooping as he flung away from her in an effort to control himself.

'Don't be silly,' she said mildly. 'It's just that I don't feel like making love tonight. Love should be an enjoyable luxury to a single woman. Wives have to put up with being mauled. Do you mind?'

'No,' he said tautly. 'I'm not a bloody animal, Gilda.'

She smiled. 'You do look smart. Where did you get it?'

He preened himself a little. She had noticed the suit. Some of his good humour returned. 'I had it made-to-measure at Keaton's. It cost me fifty-two ten.'

'You do splash it around, don't you?'

'That's the way to get more,' he said. 'More to spend on you.' He chuckled, an eye gleaming ecstatically. 'Big changes are due. Next week you and me are going to fly out to the south of France for what the big-wigs call an extended vacation in more salubrious climes.'

Gilda went to the settee and sat down.

Then she threw back her head and held herself so that her breasts stood out firmly under the silk that covered them. 'Are you serious, Dave?' she asked narrowly. 'I know you've been on about this for a long time. You've been up to something today, haven't you?'

He gave her a superior grin. 'Of course I'm serious. We'll be off on Tuesday at the latest.'

'The south of France?'

'Jugoslavia, Italy, the Isles of Greece — Turkey, if you like. Just say the word.'

'And you'll wave your wand?' Gilda drew on her cigarette and inhaled so deeply that the pupils of her eyes dilated. 'You must be really in the money.'

'So — so,' he said modestly, though his eyes said things that weren't so modest.

'All right,' she said warily. 'I shan't ask you where all this money came from.'

'Then since you're so good-mannered, I'll tell you. I had an uncle die.'

Gilda studied him a moment, her mouth spreading maliciously. 'R.I.P.' she said, blowing some ash off her lap with a sharp little puff.

Her spite stung McNally. There were moments when she took no trouble to hide the fact that she despised him. She didn't seem to understand how much he was prepared to do for her; the risks he was ready to take. She had hurt him, and he wanted to hurt her in return. 'The Queen of Hearts,' he sneered.

Gilda shrugged indifferently. 'That's another way of getting it. An honest way.'

Her readiness to accept herself as she was took the venom out of him. He felt ashamed. 'You're never going to have to get it that way again,' he said fiercely.

'Who knows what the future holds?'

'A wedding ring if you want.'

'I love you, Dave, don't I? Isn't that enough.'

'It's enough,' he said, believing her because he wanted to. He moved towards her again, his face softening into a plea.

She pressed her fingertips into her temples. 'I really do have a splitting headache.'

Bending over the back of the settee, he kissed her in the middle of the forehead. 'Better?'

'Of course,' she said archly.

McNally thrust a finger through his hair and scratched his scalp. 'Now what happens?' he asked, his eyes growing quizzical.

'You sit down,' Gilda said, patting the settee beside her.

'I don't think so,' he replied, thoughtful for a moment, then shaking his head with sudden vigour. 'Too restless. Get your glad rags on, honey, we're going out.'

'To do what?'

'The things people usually do on a Saturday evening. Dance. See a movie. Have a drink. Burn a quid or two on the wheel at Amy's. You name it.'

'How accommodating you are, Dave,' Gilda remarked, her tone edging towards cynicism.

'I wish you were,' he grinned.

'It can't be that bad.'

'It always is when I look at you.'

'Not tonight, Dave. Nothing tonight.'

He made an energetic shooing motion with his hands. 'Up you get, girl! We're going out! I won't take no for an answer!'

'I'm afraid you'll have to,' she retorted,

covering her eyes with her hands and rubbing hard. 'It's no good, Dave. Give it up. I'd only be a drag. I'm going to bed.'

Anger gusted into his throat and temples, but he fought it down. 'If you feel you must,' he said, a little too quietly.

'I do.' She looked at him gravely, her eyes unflinching.

'Fair enough,' he said. 'I'll be off, then. Got enough money?'

She nodded.

He turned away from the settee and headed for the door.

'Dave.'

He paused in reaching for the door-knob and glanced over his shoulder. 'What?'

Gilda pushed herself to her feet. She walked to a corner of the room near the record player and the television table. She reached her big, hand-tooled crocodile-skin handbag down from a shelf, and opened it. 'I've got a complimentary ticket to the Rex,' she said. 'Gina Morris gave it to me. She's an usherette, you know. They get two complimentaries a week. Here.' She held the blue ticket out to him.

McNally sauntered back to her. He looked at the ticket for a moment, smiled to himself, shrugged, and took it. 'Waste not, want not.' He clicked his heels and gave a Teutonic bow. 'Dankeschön, Fraulein Gilda.'

'Go and buy some more phrase books,' Gilda taunted. 'You'll need more than that next week. How's your French?'

'Haven't got any.' He sauntered back to the door. 'It's the worst of being brought up bloody ignorant. See you tomorrow.'

'In the afternoon,' she agreed. 'Good night.'

He passed out of the flat, pausing to shake his head behind the door. Then he followed the corridor to the stairs, trotted down them, hurried along the hall to the main door, and slowed as he walked down the steps outside it. He looked up at the darkening sky above the block then, his mouth twisting, he gazed at the cinema ticket which he still held in his hand. Suddenly he bent forward and dropped it through the iron grille that covered a drain. So much for Gilda and her contrariness. Who wanted to go to the Rex anyway? The place had long ago degenerated into a flea pit, and Saturday night was the time of advanced slap and tickle on the back row. Not that slap and tickle wasn't fine if you had somebody to slap and tickle with. After the stresses of the day, he needed something to calm him. If Gilda wouldn't do it, he must turn to alcohol. He'd go and get a drink.

He walked along Jutland Street until he came to the sea front. The Keystone Pier was showing its lights, and music came from it. A soft purple shadow lay between the sky and ocean, and spilled forward on to the sands and advancing foam. The day would soon be over; the gulls sobbed for it, and the sea mourned in its booming monotone. McNally slouched morosely along the promenade. Perhaps Gilda knew him too well. Perhaps he had given her his big talk once too often. There was still tonight. He wouldn't be rich until after tonight. So much could go wrong. He hadn't considered it before. A sense of panic filled him, and he felt the sweat on his palms and brow. If only he had already lived through tonight. He passed quivering fingertips across his forehead. A drink; he must have that drink.

Almost blundering along, he entered one of the posh new bars that faced the sea. He hated the pretentious places normally. They had been built to accommodate whores and clip holiday-makers. Vaguely annoyed by his own lack of principle, he passed through an inner door of chromium and glass and moved across a plushy lounge, where soft lighting suffused the muted colouring of a décor that might have originated on another planet. Piped music and slowly turning mirrors added to the atmosphere of hypnotic repose, and the people present talked in the lowest of voices and drank as if in respect for the dead.

McNally ordered a pint of Worthington. He carried it to the back of the room, where he had a dim view of the street through another glass-panelled door, and sat down on a strip of foam-seating. He tipped up his beer and drank greedily; then he crouched forward, with the mug between his hands, and let his ears accustom to what conversation was going on in the place. He soon realized that, as he had thought might be the case by this time, the main topic was the robbing of the A.S.E. armoured car and the killing of the guard. He listened, his thoughts groping analytically, and was disconcerted to discover that the strongest feeling present was that of surprise: surprise that such a crime could happen in Eastport. One of the speakers openly admitted that, had it not been for the murder, he would have been prepared to applaud the daring of the robbers; but as it was — and he still spoke dispassionately — the killers should be caught and hanged from the first tree. McNally shuddered at the idea, but it contained a rough justice that his own hard nature grudgingly accepted. He swallowed the rest of his beer to ease an imagined constriction of his windpipe, then stepped up to the bar — wondering what the chubby-cheeked speaker would say if he knew with whom he was rubbing shoulders — and ordered a second pint.

Sipping the beer, he returned to his

seat and sat down again. At that moment he saw the street door open. A chunky, snub-nosed man, with black hair creamed slickly over a bullet head, came in, ambled up to the bar, his double-breasted jacket hanging open in a fashion ten years out-moded, and ordered a double whisky. McNally's eyes watched the back of the newcomer's skull and inquired. The man placed an elbow on the bartop, and gazed into the mirror behind the spirit optics. Suddenly his reflected gaze met McNally's. He frowned as McNally frowned; then, turning with his drink in his hand, he slowly advanced towards the strip of foam-seating. Gradually, McNally's features relaxed into a wry smile, and then the newcomer smiled also. He lowered himself on to the seat beside McNally and softly exclaimed: 'Of all the pubs in town!'

'We both have to pick the same one,' McNally agreed. 'We'd better make this short and sweet, Herb. We mustn't be seen together by anybody that matters. Not tonight.'

'That's a chance in a thousand

anyhow,' said Setters, the screwsman, comfortably. 'Where's that little blonde brahma of yours?'

'She's got the megrimes.'

'Sometimcs they will, sometimes they won't,' Setters observed philosophically. 'My old woman is no better than the rest. Don't ever marry one, Dave.'

'Just catch me!' McNally said grimly, taking another good pull at his tankard.

'Don't swallow too much of that stuff,' Setters chuckled, a faint note of anxiety behind the jest.

'I don't think I could,' McNally boasted. 'I was born with a thirst, and the capacity to match — just like my old man. The old lady could swallow her drop, too. Blood tells.'

Setters nodded, and sipped ruminatively at his whisky. 'It's a long time to two o'clock, boy.'

'So it is,' McNally agreed. 'Is that the best time for screwing a safe?'

'The most obvious — and the best. The world has to go bye-byes, and the coppers always get the blues during the graveyard watch. It tickles you to death to see them sometimes. Just standing there like wet weeks, or huddled up in somebody's corner, like a right bloody steamer on the randy, having a drag at a butt-end. Don't worry about the busies, boy. I'll steer you clear of them.'

'No sweat,' McNally assured him.

They paused and drank again, ostensibly casual acquaintances passing a few words.

Then Setters said: 'It went all right, then?'

'Like a charm.'

'Who was the pistolero?'

'He whose name may not be spoken.'

'That ponce!'

'Ponce is right.'

'It's been given out on the News that the coppers have reason to believe that the, er, crooks have flown to the Continent. An abandoned car was found at Burgh airfield.'

'That's what they were meant to believe.'

'You sound uncertain.'

'I've heard Blessingay is on the case.'

'He's a pig-headed old basket, if ever there was one!' Setters agreed. 'He lagged me once. They ought to've pensioned him off years ago.'

'He's not as old as all that, you know.'

'See what hard living does for you?'

'His kind go on for ever. This time he's got a hell of a job on. But he's had that before.'

'Several times. Drink?'

'No thanks, Herb.'

'Well, Dave, you were here first. I'm off when I've swallowed this drop.' Setters raised his glass to his lips, then lowered it again. 'Was it all there?'

McNally rolled his eye and nodded at the bottom of his tipping tankard. 'We went to Pleasure Land, the boss and me, after the job. We went into the little knocked up office of his near the donkey engine.'

'The one where I did our diversionary screwing job a fortnight ago?'

'That's right. We opened the casket in there. Whew!'

'Luverly!' Setters finished his whisky at a gulp. 'You're sure he took the stuff home? He didn't leave it at Pleasure Land?'

'No, our scheming worked. He's taken it home and put it in his safe there.'

'Good. If he did but know it, that old iron box of his down at Pleasure Land is far harder to screw than the modern Wilcox you say he's got in his house. I'll be in there in two minutes.'

'The faster the better!' McNally muttered, his eyes suddenly fixing and his mouth thinning apprehensively. 'Don't look now; not towards the door.'

'Eh?' Setters looked and sounded startled.

'It's all right. He's gone. Of all the dirty luck!'

'Who was it?' the cracksman asked tautly.

'Ritchie Fairclough. He looked inside. I don't think he saw you. Me, I can't tell about.'

'Ritchie, eh?' Setters growled, biting his lower lip. 'That little sod doesn't miss much. He's done eye-eye duty in Greyfriars and Whitechapel. One glance is usually enough. Well, Davey?'

'Do we go on with tonight, you mean?'

'Two and two make four.'

'*Only* if he recognized you,' McNally said. 'It's tonight or never. He won't keep the stuff in his house a second night. It's due in Sheffield on Monday. This is the sort of chance that comes but once. We mustn't pass it up — whatever the risk!'

'That's my sort of thinking,' Setters said simply. 'I'm off. Don't forget the rendezvous. My backyard at half past one. Okay?'

'Okay.' McNally got slowly to his feet. He watched the screwsman leave the bar. A thousand to one chance, eh? Setters had been far too generous with the odds. Whatever Fairclough had or had not seen mustn't be allowed to matter now, but his presence at the door had been a warning. McNally felt some sort of psychic thrill down his spine. This business was going to go wrong. Somehow it was going to go wrong. The knowledge hammered his brain to a pulp. He fought it with every kind of ridicule, but the torment remained. Then he lurched over to the bar and shoved his tankard towards the barman. 'Bitter,' he snarled, daring any sort of retort or comment on his tone of voice.

His tankard filled again, McNally returned to his place by the wall. He folded his arms and sat brooding. Then he noticed one of the town's better class whores watching him from the lower end of the bar. She was blonde, curvaceous, and the fluttering picture of innocence: all eyes and red lips; a real peach. McNally had heard the boys speak of her, now he came to think about it. Myra Somebody-or-the-Other. She was fresh in from the West End to minister to the needs of the American oilmen who did the prospecting in the North Sea. But she had her moments of patriotism, too. If an Englishman was attractive to her, and could afford her, she would sometimes make herself available. McNally was flattered as he realized that the girl had just placed him in this privileged group. He was tempted to introduce himself with the Vodka and orange for which she was waiting. But there was no longer any sense of fun in him, and alcohol had blunted his desire. Besides, the girl was too like and yet unlike Gilda. He was startled to discover that he actually wanted to be faithful to Gilda. The idea of climbing into bed with another woman seemed positively distasteful to him. What on earth was wrong with him? Was he a bit drunk? It was all Gilda — Gilda! He had never been so hopelessly stuck on a girl before.

He drank part of his beer then, on a sudden impulse, got up and walked towards the door, ignoring the blonde as he passed her. Outside the bar, the darkness had settled, and a velvet veil pricked by a thousand stars had covered the sea. Away from the lights, the night would be a dark one. Thank God for that! Aside from the needs of the job that had to be done later, he liked the darkness. It covered a man and his deceit; it hid the ugliness of things. In the darkness a man's face could wear the ache and sadness of his heart; he could be himself. Living in the light was a weariness to the spirit: an abomination to the inner darkness which was gradually permeating his being.

Again he sauntered along the front. He reached the lower end of King Street, and turned into it. Just over the corner he met the narrow-shouldered and bird-faced figure of Ritchie Fairclough. The little crook was lounging against a lampstandard. He had an Evening News open between his hands, but his crafty eyes weren't upon it. Without actually glancing up, Ritchie gave McNally a faint grin of recognition and said in a voice not much above a whisper: 'How's my boy? There's you standing there, and there's me loungin' here. We're supposed to be lapping it up in Gay Paree.'

McNally let out a snort, and gazed along the street. For Saturday night, it was almost deserted. 'Christmas Day in the workhouse.'

Fairclough folded up his newspaper and tucked it underneath his arm, sergeant major fashion. 'You know what you can do wiv your Christmas pudding, me old china!'

'Serve it to John Blessingay.'

'S'right, old son. Wiv strychnine. Where for?'

'There and back.'

'Want a pint?'

McNally peered closely at Fairclough's

face, but he read nothing in it that shouldn't be there. Perhaps Ritchie hadn't seen him and Setters in the bar. 'No — no, thanks. I've had three already.'

'On the front?'

What did you make of a question like that? McNally nodded.

'That's no place for a wide-boy to go boozing. They skin you alive. How about us hunting up a pair of tarts? Nice pair of well-dressed sisters?'

'I just turned down a bang at Myra What's-her-Name?'

'So long!' Fairclough said with a derisive flap of his palm. 'Myra Shaw. You turned her down? You're sick, David boy, you're sick!' The little crook shrugged himself off the lampstandard, walked briskly across the road, his head shaking all the time, and entered a noisy bar.

McNally carried on along the street. He felt no rise in his spirits. Perhaps Fairclough had been right. Maybe he was sick. Anyhow, he knew what he was going to do next. He was going home. It had been a punishing day. He needed a couple of hours kip. There was no point in wandering the streets aimlessly and tiring himself out completely. Tired men bungled jobs, and bunglers got caught. Whatever happened, he mustn't bungle anything tonight.

But fear still ate at his brain.

6

McNally reached Culliner Street about five minutes later. The block of flats in which he lived showed few lights. He went in at the front entrance and passed along the dimly lighted hall. He saw nobody while moving towards his own door at the centre of the building. Taking out his key, he let himself into the flat and turned on the living-room light. He looked about him with distaste. The place needed cleaning up; but somehow he never managed to get round to it. One of these days he would really go to work with a broom and a tin of polish. But what was the good of kidding himself? He'd never get round to it. He didn't care enough. Perhaps that was the reason why the fastidious Gilda was going off him. But he couldn't worry about it. He was too damned tired.

Entering his bedroom, he stripped off his new suit, tossed it carelessly on to a chair, and threw himself on to the bed. He lay on top of the coverlet with his knees drawn up. There was still a lot of doubt and anger and tension in his mind; but gradually he relaxed and sleep began to creep up on him. As from the other side of the world, he heard a church clock strike ten. He decided he could spare three hours to slumber. Then he drifted away.

He awakened at ten to one. Sitting up, he felt stale and unrefreshed. Even after staggering to the bathroom and putting his head under the coldwater tap, he felt little better. Bleary-eyed, he returned to the bedroom and dressed himself in a blue shirt, a pair of jeans, and plimsolls; then, discovering from his wristwatch that he still had a few minutes to spare, he boiled a kettle of water and made himself a cup of strong coffee. This he gulped down, with one eye on the time, and at five past one he left the block again and hurried through the darkened streets towards the house in Bowyer Lane, where Herb Setters lived.

Silently, he let himself into Setters'

backyard through a door set in the street wall. He stood in the rectangle of darkness, breathing heavily. Feelings of unreality came and went. His life and its tribulations seemed to belong to somebody else. If only he could achieve awareness of self. He couldn't think what had come over him. Perhaps he was in for 'flu or a bad cold. Occasionally, he had known illness to bring nervous upsets with it.

Placing his hands upon his hips, McNally looked towards the stars and began to pick out the constellations; but he soon lost interest in this occupation and turned his gaze on to the darkened windows of the house. Herb was taking his time; perhaps checking his tools again — or making rash promises to his wife. McNally grinned to himself. After tonight, Setters might be able to keep even the rashest of rash promises. It was amazing what money could do.

McNally cocked an ear to the street. The night was full of small noises. A patter of paws, the coughing of a child in an upstairs room, the squeak of a cornered rat, the far-off clatter of a dustbin lid. There was no perfect silence. Then the noise of a nearby door closing caused McNally to give a start and whisper: 'Is that you, Herb?'

'It's me.' Rubber soles approached. 'Ready?'

'As I'll ever be.'

'Then it's Bellinger Place, here we come!'

The gate opened, and they passed through it. McNally followed the cracksman's dim form along the street. Setters was obviously in his element. In many places the darkness was so deep that it was almost impossible to recognize one corner from another; but the safebreaker glided through the town as if he were moving in broad daylight. He seemed to possess some sort of personal radar that warned him of the presence of late travellers or patrolling policemen. He always knew which alley or side-street to slip into to avoid being seen. McNally had been out with Setters before, but never been quite so impressed by the man's professional aplomb.

It was just on two o'clock when the two men entered Bellinger Place. One or two porch-lights were burning, and filmy glows reached out from them and touched gates and railings shrubs and garden ornamentation. The gloomy square seemed to be deserted, and McNally and Setters crossed it at a rapid tip-toe. They stopped in front of Westmayne's house, and gazed up at its black walls, while flurries of breeze brushed a sibilant murmur from a tree near the garden gate.

Then McNally felt Setters touch his arm. He followed the safebreaker's example and hopped over Westmayne's fence. After that they catfooted up to the house, rounded a corner, and moved along the wall until they came to the sitting-room window. Here Setters took out two pairs of black silk gloves. He handed one pair to his companion, and pulled his own on, while McNally was doing the same. Then the cracksman slipped a glass-cutter out of the leather tool-belt that he wore under his sweater and, after locating the position of the window-catch, used the cutter to incise the glass above it. This done, he took out a roll of sellotape and stretched a piece of it from the disc that he had marked to a point on the lower glass. Next he gave the circle of weakened glass a sharp tap with the cutter's handle, and it fell inwards to the extent which the checking tape would allow. After that Setters thrust a couple of fingers through the hole, released the catch, and pulled the window open. Then he hopped on to the sill, swung his legs into the room beyond, and disappeared. Taking a deep breath, McNally climbed into the house behind him and dropped quietly on to a carpeted floor. He sensed that Setters was standing a couple of yards away to the right. They both listened intently through the building's hush. If the break-in had been heard, they would soon know. A clock on a nearby mantelpiece ticked the seconds away. Nothing stirred. The quiet remained unbroken.

Setters switched on a pencil torch. He swept the slender beam across the floor. Avoiding the part-illumined furniture, they crept to a door opposite the window, and the screwsman grasped the handle and eased it open. McNally edged after his companion into the hall. The arched place seemed to resemble a railway tunnel in the thin probings of the pencil torch. Setters moved forward again, but faltered. McNally thought the man had forgotten the lay-out of the house. Memory could make a jumble of drawings at a time like this. But the cracksman soon made a left turn and moved confidently towards Westmayne's office.

The torchbeam passed over a small table which stood near the office door, and a shape standing on top of it materialized briefly. The sight settled slowly into McNally's imagination, and caused a kind of delayed shock to jolt him. A handbag? A big crocodile skin handbag? He had seen only the one like it. Gilda's. The light touched the bag again. There could be no mistake. The bag *was* Gilda's. She must have visited Westmayne during the evening, and left it behind her. No. No, that was too lame. He'd got to face facts. Her headache, her standoffishness — her over-quick denial when he had asked her if there was somebody else. Had she been doing him dirt with Westmayne? Was she upstairs now, sharing the man's bed? He must find out. There would be no peace for him until he knew the truth of the matter. His heart was throbbing, and he felt sick. He had lived thirty years and felt this strongly about only one woman. And that woman had to be a born wanton with an ego the size of a bus. It wasn't fair. It wasn't fair!

Fingers plucked at the front of McNally's shirt. The light shone into his face. He heard Setters breath out in a heavy rush. 'Don't freeze on me, you!' the cracksman warned, anger smouldering in his whisper.

McNally brushed the hand holding the torch aside. 'Go on!' he urged in a similar whisper.

Setters turned. He had the office door open, and had probably been into the room. Whatever the truth of that, McNally almost bundled him into it now. The anger between them throbbed dully, then ebbed as they disciplined themselves to the work on hand.

They reached the far wall and stopped near Westmayne's desk. A smell of cigar smoke lingered in the air, and the darkness was accentuated by the presence of thick curtains drawn over the window. Setters swept the pencil torch back and forth. The light slashed over a lot of oak panelling, a couple of bookshelves, filing cabinets, a lithograph, and a rickety table that held a typewriter. Setters stretched to the wall beside the table, pinch-gripped a small protrusion, and caused a largish section of the panelling to swing outwards on a hinge. He pushed the light into the aperture beneath, and grunted his satisfaction as the face of a safe was revealed. Then he switched off the pencil torch, thrust it into his pocket, and took out a far larger one, which he switched on and handed to McNally, who dutifully shone the beam on the numbered dials of the safe. Next the cracksman pulled a stethoscope from behind his belt and clipped it into his ears, then held it's end over the steel-guarded mechanism of the door he had to open. After that he began slowly to dial the numbers around the lock, and to listen to the clicking of tumblers and the lining up of springs. Finally, perhaps three minutes later, there was a sharper click than anything heard before, and the safe door opened as he pulled it. 'See?' Setters boasted. 'Nothing to it.'

Though McNally's thoughts were still in a turmoil of bitterness and mistrust, he experienced a moment of pleasurable anticipation as he peered into the safe. The light from the torch brought a glorious sparkle from many jewels. He put a hand into the cavity, while his companion unrolled a nylon sack. Then he started to extract the pieces of jewellery as Setters held the neck of the sack open for him. Two necklaces and a brooch fell from view; then came bracelets, pendants, gloves medallions, pectorals, a gem-encrusted turban, and a number of singly mounted jewels; all fell in a coruscating stream of whites and blues, greens, and carmine reds; a vast fortune in diamonds, emeralds, sapphires, rubies, and the purest intaglio art; a fortune such as few men were permitted to see, and only a handful in a century to own.

McNally watched Setters pull tight the sliding noose at the neck of the now bulging sack. The job was done. They turned away from the safe. It remained only to leave the house. There would be no difficulty in that. Yet McNally felt no sense of elation. His responses had gone numb again. He simply had to know whether or not Westmayne had company in bed. He must go upstairs and find out before he left the house.

They re-entered the hall. Setters was using the pencil torch again. The light was little enough; but as the cracksman glided towards the sitting-room, McNally turned to the right and tip-toed to the base of the stairs. He still had the big torch in his hand, and switched it on once more. With its bright ray playing widely before him, he went swiftly up the carpeted steps and reached the landing above. He smelled scent; attar of jasmine. This was proof enough of Gilda's presence, but he still had to see. Yes, he wanted it over. Where did the line between sanity and madness lie?

He followed his nose to a door on the right. Carefully, he opened it. Shifting sideways into the gap, he shone his light across the bedroom. The beam settled on the foot of a double bed. He let it travel towards the rumpled top of the coverlet. He saw Gilda's outflung arm, and then her face, which was twisted away from the pillow and looked almost as white as the linen beneath it. Then he saw one bared breast, and Westmayne's dark head resting on the other. At that moment the girl stirred in her sleep, smiled, and murmured in an erotic manner as she pressed her body against the man's. There was a shifting of unseen hands, and a creaking of springs. The couple appeared to be awakening. McNally stepped back on to the landing. So much for that. He knew the worst. But the irony of it. For Gilda's sake, he had betrayed Westmayne, while the girl had been doing him dirt with the same man. There was justice in it; he couldn't deny the justice. Yet it made him wonder if God was a cynic.

Turning, he crossed the landing and hurried down the stairs. He no longer cared all that much if he made a noise. The pair above wouldn't hear him; he was sure of that. Moving into the sitting-room, he turned off the big torch and went straight to the window; and cocking a leg over the sill, he dropped back to the ground, where Setters instantly appeared at his side and gave his shoulder a rough little shake. 'Where the flipping hell have you been?' the screwsman hissed angrily. 'Did you go upstairs?'

'Yes,' McNally confessed.

Setters gave vent to blasphemy. 'Why?'

'I thought I heard something,' McNally answered, a sense of the deepest personal inadequacy forcing the lie from him.

'Is that straight?' Setters asked suspiciously.

'Straight up.'

'Well, did you — hear anything?'

'Westmayne must have turned over in bed.'

'I ought to black your eye! We've taken risks enough!'

'For tonight,' McNally agreed, helping

his companion with the bag of loot as they turned away from the wall and headed for the fence. 'There's another day tomorrow.'

7

Blessingay stopped his car outside the Police Station. Mouth twisted, he set the handbrake with the kind of tug which caused the ratchet to grate its protest. Then he switched off the engine, and sat glaring through the window at the rain that was driving along the street and rising at the gutter-edges in clouds of grey spray that turned dismally in the wind. Sunday morning at eight o'clock, and not a mother's son in sight. Who'd be a copper? Everybody else was still snoring in bed. Lucky devils! But did they know it? No! Forty hours a week, regular meals, and a whole weekend to themselves. But were they satisfied? No! All men were good for these days was strike, strike, strike, and mucking the nation about generally. A spell in the Force would do a lot of them good. A hundred and twenty hours a week, grub when you could get it, no overtime, all criticism and no praise, and a few hours oblivion every other night. Just the stuff to hand the malcontents. One good dose, and they'd be happy to get Britain moving again. A nation of perishing namby-pambies, that's what the British were becoming.

The chief inspector pulled up the collar of his raincoat. He kicked open the door beside him. With a growl of resolution, he stepped out into the rain and screwed up his face as cold and stinging droplets battered into it. Then he turned his back on the weather and moved off down the street. A sudden twinge of pain caught him in the middle of the back. Surely not that! He pressed a hand to the critical area, and tried to walk faster as a remedial measure. These damned changes in the weather. Yesterday the temperature had been in the upper seventies, but during the night it had dropped twenty degrees. No wonder his lumbago was grumbling. He'd just have to hope it wouldn't develop. But if it did, he'd have to work through it, the same as usual.

He turned in at a newsagent's door. A single light burned above a slanting tray of magazines, paperbacks, and Sunday newspapers. Thank heavens one man was up and doing! Not that Blessingay had any love for the newsagent himself. Quite the contrary. The man, scrawny and small, with bright, impertinent eyes, a liverish complexion, and grey, thinning hair, stood back from the light and wished his customer a fawning 'good morning'.

'Good morning, Alfred,' Blessingay said.

'News of the World and the People?'

Blessingay nodded.

'I see Eastport has got on the front page,' the newsagent remarked, his tone a distinctly leading one. 'Your name is mentioned, Chief Inspector.'

'Those oafs have got to write something,' Blessingay said disdainfully, as he rolled up his newspapers and pushed them into his pocket. Then he ran an eye over the tobacco shelf behind the shopkeeper. 'An ounce of Empire, please.'

The packet of pipe tobacco was passed to him, and he tendered a ten shilling note, which the newsagent turned over and over before opening the till. 'Will you get them?' he asked.

'Of course,' Blessingay said gruffly.

'Such valuable jewels. A quarter of a million's worth, they say.' The newsagent tut-tutted unctuously. 'Makes you wonder what the world is coming to.'

'Murder isn't very nice either,' the chief inspector commented, looking carefully over his change.

'Oh, yes; there was somebody killed, wasn't there? An Express guard or somebody.'

'Or somebody,' Blessingay grated, turning away and reaching for the doorhandle as Sergeant Logan swept in off the street and sent the door shuddering inwards with a powerfully thrusting hand.

'Good morning, sir,' the sergeant said breezily. 'A nice rain to make things grow.'

'You've shot up a couple of inches overnight,' the chief inspector observed, sniffing. 'What do you want here?'

'My newspaper, sir.'

'The man reads,' Blessingay said to the floor. 'Do hurry up, sergeant.'

'Flap on, sir?' Logan asked, taking and paying for a rather more augustly named Sunday newspaper than those which found favour in his superior's strictly plebian eye.

'There's always a flap on around me,' Blessingay retorted. 'Ready?'

'At the double, sir.'

'Jump to it, then!' Blessingay nodded curtly to Alfred, then led the way out to the street, where he pulled his chin into his collar, stuffed his hands into his pockets, and launched himself into the slanting rain, the crown of his Homburg tipped forward to meet it.

'Lumbago, sir?' Logan asked in knowing but sympathetic tones, as he matched the older man stride for stride.

'Not quite,' Blessingay answered brusquely, an unseen grin wrinkling the corner of his mouth. 'I've got the hump, Logan. Black and blue, Kipling said, didn't he? Well, mine's all black; a nasty sooty black, quite unrelieved and stamped chief inspectors only. This blasted weather, Sergeant! Do you like working Sundays?'

'No, sir,' Logan replied emphatically, 'I don't.'

'You know your trouble, don't you?' Blessingay snapped. 'You're too honest to be a policeman. Have you been in yet?'

'Yes and no, sir,' Logan answered. 'I parked my car down by the mews, then walked straight through the Station. But I didn't see anybody. It pays to get your paper first. Old Johnson is usually sold out by ten o'clock.'

'Detective Sergeants,' Blessingay said severely, as he turned through the entrance to the Police Station, 'are not supposed to read in the Firm's time.'

'Only the News of the World and the People?' Logan asked innocently, as they walked along the passage which led to the heart of the building.

Blessingay pushed open the glass doors that gave access to the duty room. 'Oh, they're highly educational,' he said seriously. 'Morning,' he greeted, scowling at the desk sergeant. 'I heard you were dead, Wilkes.'

'No such luck, sir,' the healthily plump and rubicund Wilkes replied, looking up from a number of forms that he was pinning together. 'Good for thirty years yet.'

'That's it,' Blessingay agreed, pulling a face as his back gave him another slight twinge. 'We'll both go to Logan's funeral. How about a nice inexpensive bunch of dandelions between us?' He paused, frowning and snapping his fingers as he began to concentrate. 'Cars, cars. We seemed to have dozens of them yesterday. Have the fingerprints boys come up with anything useful?'

'No, sir,' the desk sergeant replied. 'The reports are lying on your desk. We've traced the owners of the cars.'

'Any help there?'

'Mr. Bryant didn't think so, sir,' Wilkes answered.

'If that's what he thinks,' Blessingay said grudgingly, 'then that's how it is. No sign of Messrs. Reith and Gedge yet, I suppose?'

'No, sir. They seem to have ducked right out of the district. It may take a day or two.'

'Yes, it may. Anything else?'

Wilkes replied in the negative. He began moving towards a telephone which had started ringing at the other end of the desk. He picked the receiver up and put it to his ear. He listened as a female voice gabbled away in the diaphragm, twice tried to get a word in edgeways, then resigned himself to letting the spate expend itself. At long last he managed to say: 'Yes, madam. I have it all, thank you. The address is Bellinger Place? Good. Thank you. Yes. There will be an officer along to see you as soon as possible, madam.' The phone clattered back to rest, and Wilkes sighed and ran a finger around the inside of his collar.

'What was all that about?' Blessingay demanded, trying to work up a genuine interest.

'A burglary, by the sound of it, sir,' the sergeant replied. 12 Bellinger Place. The home of Mr. Gerald Westmayne.'

'Westmayne?' The chief inspector pondered a second or two. 'Would that be the Westmayne who owns Pleasure Land?'

'That's right, sir,' Wilkes replied.

'Who was the lady?'

'Mr. Westmayne's housekeeper, sir. Mrs. Teresa Sanderman.'

'And so?'

'It seems Mrs. Sanderman spent the night at her sister's place, sir, on the other side of the town. When she got back to her employer's house, a short while ago, she found that one of the sitting-room windows had been broken open. Then she went straight into Mr. Westmayne's office and discovered that the safe had been robbed.'

'The gist?'

'That's it, sir.'

'Is Mr. Westmayne at home?'

'Couldn't say, sir. Probably not.'

'Why probably not?'

'The woman ringing up seems to suggest — '

'I take your point, Wilkes. But the favoured classes sleep late on Sunday morning. You'd think she would've wakened him, though.' Blessingay scratched the tip of his nose. 'Not important, I suppose. It looks like ours, Logan. We're the only C.I.D men on duty. Fit?'

'I could answer that, sir,' Logan said,

grinning as he faced about.

'Don't,' Blessingay advised. 'It's Sunday, I know, but I'm not feeling that charitable.'

They retraced their steps along the passage and left the Police Station. With the rain still pouring about them, they got into the chief inspector's car, and with a quick glance into his mirror, Blessingay pulled away from the curb. Circumnavigating the town centre, he drove into one of Eastport's older residential areas, checked at a couple of crossroads, and passed into Bellinger Place, where the tall grey houses pushed their slate roofs and high brick chimneys into the illusory film of light which the downpour formed about them. Blessingay peered through his windscreen distastefully. If he were sometimes weak and human enough to envy the rich their homes, this particular section of the wealthy was not among them. He would as soon live in a graveyard as Bellinger Place. 'Number twelve, isn't it, Logan?' he asked, already slowing to a stop before a garden gate which wore that number.

'Yes, sir,' Logan confirmed. 'Mrs.

Teresa Sanderman.'

Blessingay nodded. He got out of the car, hunched himself up as he walked round the bonnet, and walked to the gate, which Logan had already reached and opened for him. He strode up to the front door, and stood aside while Logan rang the bell. The door opened the instant the ringing stopped, and Blessingay was convinced that the dark woman who had appeared in the entrance had been standing behind it all the time. 'Police, madam,' he said.

'Please come in,' the woman invited.

Blessingay removed his hat and stepped into the hall. He glanced about him quickly, then inched forward to let Logan join him. The woman closed the door behind them and said: 'Through here, please, gentlemen.' And stepping ahead of them, she led the way into a room almost opposite the stairs. 'This is where they came in.'

'They?' the chief inspector queried.

The woman shrugged. 'They — he; I don't know.'

'I see.' Blessingay kept his hands in his

pockets as he moved across the room and had a look at the circle of glass which had been removed from the pane above the window-catch. 'The usual,' he said to Logan. 'A glass-cutter and a strip of sellotape. You can see it on at the pictures any day of the week.'

'Looks professional enough,' Logan commented, studying the floor for any trace of footmarks.

'No doubt,' Blessingay agreed. 'We'll leave it to the dabs specialists again. But I'll be surprised if there's anything to show out there, on the window or beneath it. This rain.' He smiled frostily at the woman. 'You are Mrs. Sanderman?'

'Yes.'

'I'm Detective Chief Inspector Blessingay, and this is Detective Sergeant Logan. Show us the safe, please.'

'If you'll come into the office?' Mrs. Sanderman led them out into the hall, then across it and into a room on the right, where she went at once to a section of panelling which stood open on the far wall. 'Here.'

Blessingay cast a casual glance across

the desk and other office furniture present as he made for the spot. He peered deep into the empty safe, studied its door a moment, then turned to Logan with an eyebrow raised. 'Nothing of the Simon Pure about that, I must admit.'

'He knows his stuff, sir.'

'Or they?'

Logan smiled thinly. 'Or they.'

The chief inspector turned to the woman now. 'Any idea what was inside it?'

Mrs. Sanderman clasped and unclasped her hands. 'No.'

Blessingay took his first good look at her. She was tall for a woman, raven-haired, sloe-eyed, and strong featured, with a throat as firm and unmarked as new ivory. He supposed she would be about thirty-six or seven. Still in her good years. And what sex-appeal she radiated! No healthy man could withstand such magnetism for long. Housekeeper? Blessingay smiled inwardly. Well, yes; but he'd lay a fiver she was also Westmayne's mistress. 'We have to prove the existence of the stolen property,' he explained, 'before we can prove larceny.'

'I understand,' the woman said.

'Is Mr. Westmayne away for the weekend?'

'No.' Mrs. Sanderman looked surprised.

'Then where is he?'

'Upstairs in bed.'

Blessingay remembered his recent dialogue with the desk sergeant, and exchanged glances with Logan. 'Am I to take it you haven't told Mr. Westmayne about any of this?'

The housekeeper's face became wooden. 'I didn't want to disturb him. He needs his rest. He's had a lot of worry lately.'

'Worry?'

'Business problems, I think. But I oughtn't to be discussing his affairs, ought I? A good housekeeper should keep her nose out of things. It's really the first rule, isn't it? The trouble is, you can't help feeling for a man when he's down. There was that other business too — ' Mrs. Sanderman caught herself, and lowered her eyes, as if she had become aware that she was beginning to run on.

'What other business?' Blessingay prompted.

'Oh, perhaps I shouldn't — '

'What other business?' the chief inspector insisted.

'Somebody tried to rob the safe in Mr. Westmayne's office at the amusements ground.'

'Pleasure Land? When was this?'

'About two weeks ago, sir. It worried Mr. Westmayne very much.'

'Did it? We heard nothing about it.'

'He didn't want to make trouble. Mr. Westmayne is such a thoughtful man.'

'That,' Blessingay commented, 'is a matter of opinion. You believe robbery has been committed here, don't you?'

'Of course. Why else would I ring the Police Station?'

'Do you feel the present robbery is related to the abortive one at Pleasure Land?'

'I — I suppose so. Yes.'

'You think that somebody is after some specific thing?'

'His money, I imagine,' the woman answered.

'That's not quite what I mean.'

'I know it isn't.'

'Please answer me properly, then.'

'But I don't know. It's the job of the Police — your job — to find out, isn't it?'

'Yes,' Blessingay admitted, glancing towards the ceiling. 'I'm afraid we shall have to get that most considerate master of yours out of his bed, Mrs. Sanderman. Will you see to it, please?'

'Surely it can't be necessary!' she protested, a tremble in her voice betraying the apparent restraint and protectiveness she wished to emphasize.

Blessingay began to wonder; there was a lot about the woman that didn't ring true. But he kept his patience and said: 'Only Mr. Westmayne can tell us what was in his safe. Correct?'

Crestfallen, she nodded.

'Then get him up, will you, please?'

Her rather beautiful face suddenly lighted up. 'I've got an idea,' she said. 'Why don't we go up to him in his bedroom? Then he won't have to get up.'

For an instant Blessingay felt inclined to give her a piece of his mind. But then he sensed that something deeper than Westmayne's well-being lay behind the woman's suggestion. What exactly was

155

her game? He'd play along. It was the only way to find out. 'Whatever you wish,' he said gruffly. 'Lead on. Let's go, Logan.'

They followed her out of the room, to the right, and up the stairs; then across the landing, where a faint smell of perfume permeated the heavy air, and up to a bedroom door. Mrs. Sanderman knocked gently and called: 'Mr. Westmayne! Are you awake, please?'

'What — what . . . ?' spluttered a startled male voice from the room beyond. 'Teresa?' The voice accused now, and was angry. 'Is that you?'

'Yes,' the woman answered.

'Damn you!' Westmayne exclaimed. 'How dare — Who's that with you?'

'The Police,' Blessingay broke in. 'Your house was burgled last night. Your safe has been opened. I'd like to know what was in it. Will you come downstairs, or would you prefer us to come in?'

'Why — why . . . '

Mrs. Sanderman appeared to interpret this spluttering as an invitation to enter. She opened the bedroom door and pushed it back against the inner wall.

Blessingay had a good view of the bed on the other side of the room. He saw Westmayne, bleary-eyed, crumple-cheeked, naked, and black jowled, sitting up in bed. He also saw a woman bent forward beside the man, her blonde hair falling loose over her face and her bare breasts spilling out across the top of the coverlet. Then, with the speed of fright and outraged modesty, she threw her torso backwards and went wriggling out of sight beneath the bedclothes, where she lay as a motionless hump, apparently trying to persuade herself and everybody else that she was not there at all. Mrs. Sanderman's face twisted spitefully, but there was a generally embarrassed silence. Blessingay broke this when he quietly said: 'Please show your face again, miss — or is it missus? There's no need to be shy.'

The blonde's head slowly reappeared. Her shoulders came next, and then she cowered back against the bedrails, with a sheet pulled up under her chin. 'Miss,' she mumbled.

'I take it you don't live here,' Blessingay said comfortably. 'We'd better have your name and address. These things help keep our business tidy, you know.'

The girl hesitated. She turned a pleading eye on the man beside her.

'Tell him!' Westmayne snapped.

One of the blonde's shoulders flinched involuntarily. 'Gilda Kemp. Flat eighteen, Parker House, Jutland Street.'

'Thank you, Miss Kemp,' the chief inspector said, throwing a quick glance at Logan, who was scribbling in his notebook. 'I suppose you heard nothing suspicious during the night?'

'No,' the blonde replied shortly.

'I didn't imagine you would have,' Blessingay commented. 'Well, Mr. Westmayne? I'm sure the same applies to you. Out you get, sir.'

'Why?'

'Come downstairs and see your empty safe. The better to remember what you had in it.'

'But I'm — I'm . . . ' Westmayne spluttered hopelessly.

Mrs. Sanderman walked into the room. She picked up a dressing-gown which was lying near the foot of the bed. Without saying a word, she tossed the robe to

158

Westmayne, after which she turned and walked disdainfully back to the landing.

Westmayne went through a good many contortions in order to hide his hairy nakedness as he slipped the garment on. Then he got out of bed and crossed to the door. 'You called them in!' he snarled at his housekeeper, the congestion in his cheeks and the glare in his eyes suggesting that he could no longer hold the words back.

'Of course,' the woman agreed innocently.

'It's unnecessary. Absurd!'

'Why?' Blessingay asked softly.

'You did say the safe was empty?'

The chief inspector picked up a cunning glint in the other's eyes, and realized he'd made a mistake. 'Yes.'

'Well that's how it ought to be. That's how I left it.'

'Did you break into your own house, sir?'

'Don't be bloody ridiculous!' Westmayne stormed. 'Kids, I expect. The little perishers are always up to some mischief or the other round here!'

'I expect the same lot of children tried to rob the safe in your office at Pleasure Land.'

Westmayne looked at the dark woman as if he could murder her. 'Your filthy great mouth!' he exploded. 'I can't call my soul my own!'

'Is that any way to speak to a woman who has served you so faithfully?' Blessingay wondered. 'You ought to apologize at once.'

'I'll see her in hell!' Westmayne declared vindictively. 'You're wasting your time here — '

'Blessingay, Chief Inspector.'

'I know who you are,' Westmayne answered truculently, though his manner changed for the better almost at once. 'I also know you're only doing your duty. But it should be plain to you, after what I've said, that some poor fool of a thief has had a night's work for nothing.' He paused, his expression heavy with grievance. 'I put it to you. Wouldn't you be up the pole if you'd been disturbed as I've been disturbed? Mrs. Sanderman has a tendency to exceed what's expected of her. I didn't imagine she'd be home so early. But there's no law against spending the night with a girl, is there?'

'No,' the chief inspector admitted. 'But don't try to shift the issue. A crime *has* been committed here, and it will *have* to be investigated. The chap who screwed your safe is a professional of the best or worst sort. Now professionals are careful people. They're careful not to waste their luck and their efforts. You do see what I'm driving at, don't you? I'm very surprised that our cracksman wasted his talents on an empty safe.'

'One way or another,' Westmayne said indifferently, 'it happens to us all.'

'I don't think so,' Blessingay said. 'Not twice. I haven't lost sight of the Pleasure Land job, you see. There's a lot that doesn't satisfy me here.'

'Are you accusing me of something, Chief Inspector?' Westmayne asked narrowly.

'Not yet.'

'I've good friends on the Watch Committee.'

'Threats?'

'We'll see.'

Blessingay glared at Westmayne, then he nodded to Logan and said: 'There's nothing else we can do here. We'll get them along to the Station if we need them for anything. Understand, Mrs. Sanderman? That includes you.'

'She understands,' Westmayne said, yawning negligently, though his breathing betrayed relief. 'Show them out, Teresa.'

'We can find our own way,' Blessingay said grimly, as he looked Westmayne up and down. 'I hope you can.'

Westmayne coloured distinctly, and made no reply.

8

Blessingay set the seat springs squealing as he settled his seventeen stone bulk behind the wheel of the Citroen again. He took out his pipe and tobacco pouch, loaded for a short smoke, and struck a match. 'I take it,' he said, sucking a light as Logan shut the passenger's door, 'that there are faces at the windows of number twelve?'

'You wouldn't believe,' Logan said from the corner of his mouth. 'There's the blonde upstairs, trying her darndest not to be seen. There's Westmayne behind a curtain downstairs, and Mrs. Sanderman is peeping through the letter box.'

'Guilty lot of so-and-so's,' Blessingay remarked, settling his pipe between his back teeth and easing the car back into motion.

'Guilty, sir? What of?'

'Good question,' the chief inspector said, touching the pavement with a front wheel as he followed a narrow lane out of Bellinger Place and met up with a wider street that led towards the town centre. 'What's your opinion of the Sanderman woman, Logan?'

'Black heart, black deeds. Jealous as sin, sir.'

'Yes, she was out to make him squirm. And a lot more.'

'A lot more,' Logan echoed.

'Don't stop.'

'She wants us to know something.'

'Yes.' Blessingay wagged a finger. 'On the down beat, start supposing.'

'Supposing,' the sergeant began, 'a man has been up to a few tricks he doesn't want the law to know about. Now this chap has a raven-haired, sloe-eyed, rootin'-tootin' bedpartner that he's got tired of. He's recently made a change, shall we say, and equipped himself with a much younger and very presentable blonde. The dark woman wouldn't be human if she liked this; so, being a bit on the melodramatic side, she decides to get her own back as subtly as possible. She learns that her employer and ex-lover has something of great value in his safe, so she calls in a screwsman to crack the barrel and steal the contents, which are probably already 'hot' anyway. Caught off guard, and tucked up in bed beside his new mistress, our chap is confronted by two whacking great coppers. He puts on a highly suspect performance, which the dark female, in her insidious way, has naturally anticipated and prepared us for with the hint that somebody has already tried to rob the safe in the man's office at his place of business.'

'Not bad,' Blessingay approved as the sergeant paused. 'I don't see any real flaw in your reasoning, Logan. If she wanted to get her own back on Westmayne, she naturally wouldn't do it in a manner that might boomerang at some future date. That one loves her hide. There's an arrow in all this, Logan. Where does it point?'

'The Lahkpore jewels, sir?'

'It's a possibility we can't afford to overlook.' The chief inspector deliberately missed the road on which the Police Station stood, and began to approach its farther end by a circular route. 'Tell you what. We'll assume Westmayne was mixed up in the A.S.E. robbery yesterday. We'll pretend he did put the loot in his safe, and that our cunning Mrs. Sanderman and her cracksman have now got it. Who have we got in Eastport who's man enough to screw Westmayne's safe?'

'Vance Pickard, Lew Richter, and Herb Setters.'

'Setters is one of the best in the country.'

'He is, sir,' Logan agreed; 'but he's also an ugly little blighter and no man for the women. The Sanderman party is very physical. She'd be on intimate terms with any man with whom she went into business. I'd put my money on Vance Pickard. He's tall, dark, and handsome, and he'll chase anything that wears a skirt and high heels.'

'I must admit you've got a point,' Blessingay said doubtfully. 'Anyway, if there's any truth in our game, Westmayne will feel obliged to get in touch with his fellow thieves and pass on the bad news. Something could come out of that. And then there's the Kemp girl. She might prove to be some sort of lead. Birds of a feather, as the saying goes. Ever seen her before?'

'Yes, sir. I think she used to do it for pay. I'm sure she was on our list of street-walkers.'

'But she's off the game now?'

'I can't say for certain, sir. They never retire.'

'Well, I saw W.P.S. Gilbert's name on the duty roster for today. We'll summon her into the office when we get back, Logan. The W.P.S. keep tabs on the pros. in our patch.'

'Any ideas beyond that, sir?'

Blessingay nodded slowly. Then he realized that his pipe had gone out. Removing it from his mouth, he placed it on top of the dashboard and blew a few flakes of grey ash off his chest. 'I've got something pretty definite in mind,' he said, watching water swirl along the gutters and go splashing down the drains. 'But I haven't quite decided how to handle it yet. I'll tell you all about it when I have.' With that, he made a final turn left and re-entered the street on which the

Police Station stood. Then he cruised up to the main entrance and drew to a stop.

The two men went straight through the Station to the C.I.D. room. Here they took off and hung up their wet coats and hats. Then the chief inspector went into his tiny office adjacent and switched on the intercom. 'Desk?' he asked. Wilkes? Is W.P.S. Gilbert in the building?'

'She's in her office, sir,' Wilkes replied.

'Send her through to the C.I.D. room,' Blessingay ordered.

'Very good, sir.'

Blessingay switched off the intercom, made a few tidying passes across the top of his desk, then sauntered back into the C.I.D room, where Sergeant Logan was occupying one of his favourite seats — the top of a cold radiator — and casually rolling a foot from side to side as he examined the wet toe of his shoe. The chief inspector sat down at the sergeant's desk, picked up a cheap ballpoint pen, doodled with it for a moment, then began tapping its cap on a green hold-all which contained a set of statements. There was a far away look in his eyes; but his alertness returned when a knock sounded on the door, and he stood up, put one foot on the chair which he had vacated, leaned an elbow on his raised thigh, and called: 'Come in!'

The door opened. A brown-haired policewoman wearing an immaculate uniform and sergeant's stripes entered. She stopped in front of the desk and stood dutifully to attention. Blessingay smiled at her. Not a bad-looker was the W.P.S. Oval-faced, straight-nosed, full-lipped, a good brow; all the features of beauty if only she would look less severe. It made the chief inspector wonder why she had never married. Dedicated coppers among the females of the species were rare. Still, at thirty-three or four there was still time. 'At ease, Gilbert,' Blessingay said. 'Another of the Sunday sufferers.'

The W.P.S. relaxed; her eyes smiled slightly.

'Just a question or two,' the chief inspector advised. 'Do you know a blonde by the name of Gilda Kemp?'

'Yes, sir,' the W.P.S. replied.

'A prostitute, isn't she?'

'She was, sir. I think she's being kept these days.'

'By whom?'

'A youngish man, sir. He's fairly popular among the girls of easy virtue. His name is McNally.'

'McNally? Never heard of him. What does he do?'

'He's one of these mystery men, sir. He never seems to do anything at all, but he's always got plenty of money in his pocket.'

Blessingay's bushy eyebrows twitched. 'That sounds promising. Parkhurst is full of ex-mystery men.'

'Birds of a feather?' Sergeant Logan murmured.

'The old saw begins to buzz,' Blessingay agreed. 'But we mustn't begin jumping to conclusions. What does McNally look like, Sergeant Gilbert?'

The W.P.S. answered quickly and willingly. 'A bit over middle height, sir. Good looking in a hard-featured and very masculine sort of way. Very broad shouldered and thick-limbed; the compact type. A rough handful, I'd say.'

'A rough handful.' The chief inspector's spine stiffened as he repeated the words to himself. 'That's how Constable Fuller described one of the chaps who cut the cable over at the Sporting Club. I wonder if we're on to something? Does this chap have a moustache, Sergeant Gilbert, and wear long yellow hair?'

'No, sir.' the W.P.S. replied quite emphatically. 'He has no moustache, and he wears his brown hair very short. Almost close-cropped.'

'Details,' Blessingay murmured, his eyes narrowing. 'The bits and pieces always come together in the end. Disguise may be *de trop* in some respects, Logan, but crooks still use it. Just that small change in appearance makes all the difference. I want you to pay this chap McNally a visit. Get him talking. Try to find out what he was doing yesterday afternoon. Labour it. It's almighty hard to sustain a fiction for a long time. Be a very nosy copper.' The chief inspector grinned bleakly over the adjective, and gave his full attention to the W.P.S. again. 'Any idea where

McNally lives, Sergeant Gilbert?'

'Yes, sir. The block of flats in Culliner Street.'

'Good girl,' Blessingay said. 'That'll save a bit of digging, anyway. All right, you can go. Thanks.'

The W.P.S. inclined her head, turned smartly on her heel, and marched out of the room, shutting the door quietly behind her.

'Look at that,' Blessingay said, viewing his sergeant with a wicked eye. '*Esprit de corps*, they call it.' He gestured to include the entire Station before he spoke again. 'And I've got you lot, you scruffy lot of articles!' Then he sat down again, a half grin slowly slipping from his face, and resumed tapping the cap of the ballpoint pen on the hold-all.

'Do you want me to go and interview McNally now, sir?' Logan asked uncertainly.

'Yes, Sergeant. But you can hang on a moment.' The chief inspector went on looking very thoughtful. 'I'd better tell you what I'm going to do next. I'm going to play one of my hunches, Logan. Out at

Burgh airfield we shared some talk about fences. I gave the matter a lot more thought after that and, in view of this morning's developments, I feel more strongly than ever that whoever has the Lahkpore jewels will try to get rid of them locally — and quickly.

'Now our East Anglian fences are few and far between. Those who are known don't add up to much. They're mostly go-betweens for the big chaps up in London. And the unknowns, so far as we can judge, don't handle 'hot' stuff worth a damn. But there's one man in Norwich I've always had my doubts about. Do you remember George Brenner, who used to have the jeweller's shop in King Street? Perhaps you wouldn't, though; he was before your time; he left Eastport in '51.

'We had at least two big jewel thefts in East Anglia while Brenner lived in this town, and on both occasions the evidence pointed to him as having fenced the stuff. But we never came within a mile of proving anything. I think our attentions put the wind up him, all the same, for he pulled up his stakes as soon as he decently could and scampered off. He may have been on the legit ever since; he may always have been on the legit; but one thing I'm sure about — in his business he's second to none. He'd be just the man to break up the Lahkpore jewels and change their entire appearance. I can't get his name out of my mind. The careful little man who picks and chooses. Yes, a local thief in a hurry might very well go to him.'

'Today?' Logan asked, though his shifting inflection almost changed the question into a statement.

'I said quickly, Sergeant,' Blessingay agreed. 'Big loot scares little hooks.'

'You're going to Norwich, sir?'

'Yes. Now.'

'You want to handle it alone?'

'That's the only way to handle what I've got in mind, Sergeant. I'm sticking my neck right out. If I'm right, I'm right — and toss me a bouquet. But if I'm wrong, why advertise it?' Blessingay gave a disarming grin. 'Even chief inspector's have their tawdry pride. Don't fret, Logan, I'll be in touch. If I didn't think you were capable of minding the shop, I wouldn't be leaving you. Now go and see what the gods have to offer concerning friend McNally.' The chief inspector moved towards the peg from which his raincoat hung in soggy black folds. 'For myself, I expect to be drinking a lot of tea. A wonderful stimulant tea — but such damned nuisance in other respects.'

9

McNally was glad of the warmth that met him as he stepped into the diesel unit at Eastport railway station. The rain had soaked him to the skin during his walk from Culliner Street. He felt jaded, and bereft of purpose; years older than his true age. The journey he was about to undertake was a matter of necessity, otherwise he would have shunned it in the present conditions.

Raising the battered old suitcase he carried between his hands, he pitched it on to the luggage rack, then he sat down on the seat beneath it and pushed his fingers through his wet hair, flicking droplets of water away from him in all directions. Opening his raincoat, he dried his hands by wiping them on the insides of his thighs, then he took a packet of cigarettes and a box of matches from one of his jacket pockets. Putting a damp cigarette between his lips, he fumbled the heads off three matches before managing to persuade a fourth to hiss feebly into flame, then he lighted up and inhaled to the full capacity of his lungs, tipping back his head and closing his eyes at the same time.

He'd get over it, of course. He had been foolish to set so much store by Gilda in the first place. Hadn't he always known that the girl would do him in the eye in the end? Whores were often frigid; but that had never been true of Gilda. She was sexually addicted; perhaps even the victim of an incipient nymphomania. She was a natural bed-hopper: she just had to have a change of man. Westmayne had always lusted after her. McNally remembered the man's thinly disguised glances of jealousy when he had seen them together, and he supposed that Westmayne had been visiting the girl on the quiet. Gilda liked presents, and Westmayne was generous where his interest lay, you had to say that for him. The seduction had probably been a fairly drawn out affair. McNally recalled the period during which Gilda's affections had cooled towards him, and now saw it for what it was. How could he have been such a fool as to suppose that she had been simply torturing him a little? In fact, she had wanted to be rid of him — without having to lose the amenities that he provided. Whenever possible, she had saved herself for Westmayne. My word, but that stung! McNally chewed viciously at a fragment of tobacco, and spat. Once a whore, always a whore! The lesson was well taken. He had already sworn to himself that he would never become emotionally involved over a woman again. In future, he would find them, bed them, and forget them. It was the only sensible policy which a man could adopt in his dealings with women.

The diesel unit gave a jolt and started to hum and vibrate as it moved ahead. The dark walls and wet platforms of the station began slipping backwards, then the train curved away from all cover and crossed the fringes of a marshalling yard. It began to gather speed. Rain slashed across the windows, a line of carriages and trucks blurred by, a signal box loomed and seemed to jerk from sight, and points clattered briefly. Water appeared on McNally's left; a vast expanse of it, grey and translucent, flooding away through fine mist towards faintly purpled mudbanks and a humped shoreline that caught at the low-hanging clouds and the rain which dragged beneath them. The scene was a gloomy one; the world seemed a grim and bitter place this morning.

McNally lit a second cigarette from the butt of the first. Then his upturned eyes caught sight of the suitcase through the webbing of the rack. A surge of optimism lifted him as he hit rock-bottom. He was being an ungrateful bastard. No matter how much he and Setters lost on the sale of the jewels, the suitcase held a great deal of money for them both. He would soon be able to buy himself the Mercedes that he had always wanted. And there was nothing to stop him from going to the south of France alone. Not that he would stay alone for long, of course. He would be able to enjoy every bit of the sweet life that came a rich man's way. Wine, women, and sunshine; he would revel in them. Then he would try water-skiing, aqua-lung diving, and fishing; do some sight-seeing: move on to Italy — down to Capri; take a swim into the famous blue grotto. What was good enough for Caesar was good enough for him. But not too good. He would live as a man should. Dammit all! There was no cause for his depression. What man worthy of his salt ever wasted an hour in moping? At long last, he had got the world on his side. As the Americans liked to put it, he'd got it made!

He looked out of the window once more. Now a wide tongue of land stretched between him and the water. Fields began to emerge from the broken landscape, and bridges, trees, and cottages. The hazy, sodden broadlands shifted flatly across the extremities of his vision, and lulled him. He shut his eyes, and kept them shut, and soon he was asleep.

His slumber endured to the end of the journey. He was awakened by a rough hand shaking his shoulder. His eyes opened with a start, which was followed by a sullen throbbing of anger, and he straightened in his seat, with a hand pressed to his heart. Instinctively, he shot a glance at the rack. His suitcase had disappeared, and his stomach seemed to turn over. 'Where is it?' he demanded hoarsely, only just managing to check the hand that he thrust towards the throat of the thick-shouldered guard whose fat face hung no more than a foot above his own.

'Steady on!' the man advised, frowning as he backed off and dug a thumb towards the floor. 'Is that what you're looking for?'

'Sorry,' McNally muttered, getting up and crabbing out of his seat. 'Sorry, mate.'

'I lifted it down for you,' the guard said, the apology bringing more righteous indignation than ever to his tones and expression. 'We're in Norwich, and have been for three minutes. You don't want to go back to Eastport, do you?'

'I've said sorry,' McNally snarled, elbowing the guard aside and snatching up his case, after which he went bumping and banging along the gangway until he reached the nearest vestibule, where he stepped through an open door on to a covered platform.

'Making off with the Crown Jewels, then?' the guard called, his derisive grin distorted by the jagged rivulets of rain that ran down the window against which his face was pressed.

'I'll crown you in a minute, if you don't shut up!' McNally retorted, showing his teeth as he strode towards the barrier.

He had a look at the time on the station clock. It was one p.m. He felt like a drink, but decided against it as he left the station. Alcohol would probably inflame his mood. Whenever he was awakened out of a deep sleep he had a tendency to be temperamental. If only the guard had left the case where it was. Nevertheless, he regretted his rudeness to the man; it had been uncalled for. You could never tell where these things might end. But it was done now.

With the wind blowing the rain about his ears, McNally walked over the Foundry Bridge and on by the Victorian dwellings on the right of Prince of Wales Road. He turned right near the first set of traffic lights at the top of the hill. Walking faster now, he moved into Tombland and passed the cathedral; then he crossed the road near the Cavell Memorial and approached Elm Hill corner, where he turned left and went a little further, before turning right, after which he almost lost himself in the leaning seventeenth-century world of the old city, with its narrow cobbled streets and small, flint-walled churches behind tall black railings. Near one of these churches, he turned into a recess which was occupied by a single half-timbered building, which had a sagging roof of grey tiles, lattice-work windows under the eaves, and crossbeams above a much larger window at ground level that was protected by a steel grille. The black door which gave entrance to the place looked thick and heavy enough to resist the assault of a battering ram. Above it, in Gothic lettering, a large board carried the legend GEORGE BRENNER — JEWELLER.

McNally let his steps incline towards

the shop. He stopped outside the door and cast a glance around him. The rain went on falling, but nothing else stirred. Across the street, a light burned in the window of Ye Olde Norfolke Café. A shadow was visible behind a muslin curtain. It might have been human; but, equally, it could have been thrown by a large piece of furniture. Whatever the truth, McNally saw nothing in it to worry him, and, turning to the door, he knocked on it just hard enough to send the echoes hurrying into the house beyond.

Soon he heard the scuff of approaching slippers. The door opened about three inches. A faded grey eye and a bald temple the colour of a tea-stain appeared in the gap. 'Yes?' an old voice asked, low and breathlessly.

'As per phone call. McNally.'

'You ought to have used the back door,' the old man said reproachfully.

'There's nobody about,' McNally answered impatiently. 'Don't keep me standing out here, Brenner. I'm getting soaked through and through!'

Grudgingly it seemed, the door opened

wide enough to admit a man. McNally passed through it. Standing on the mat just inside the shop, he set the suitcase down, and shook himself like a dog, taking in his surroundings as he did so. He was standing in a large, black-timbered room, with three glass display-cases standing in the form of a triangle before a glass counter that ran almost the entire width of the floor. Gems winked and sparkled everywhere in the hooded fluorescent lighting; precious metals shone. Rings, clasps, chains, talismans: there was something to suit every need or taste; but to the customer with real money in his pocket, it was obvious that Brenner, the connoisseur, offered nothing but the best. McNally nodded and grinned at the broad-backed, bent, paunchy, and bow-legged old man before him. 'Remind me to rob you one of these days,' he said.

'We shall have to see,' Brenner chuckled. 'You see forty thousand pounds worth of stock.'

'A bagatelle,' McNally laughed, lifting the suitcase and patting it. 'Out of this lot you should be able to fix yourself up for the rest of your days.'

'Good,' Brenner said, nodding. 'I've no time for scraps and oddments. They bring small rewards and long prison terms.' He used a thumbnail to pick at the dried egg on the front of his acid-stained waistcoat. 'Come through to my workshop, young man.'

McNally followed the old man through a door in the narrow piece of wall to the right of the counter. They passed along a dark, musty-smelling passage and reached a flight of wooden steps. Ascending, they came to a strut-supported platform, beyond which another door let them into a room at the back of the building. McNally turned an eye from left to right. He saw that a bench had been built into the longer wall on his left. Under the window, directly before him, stood a second bench that supported a number of clamps, some fine drills, and a tray of delicate tools. Nearer to hand, a small forge, crucibles, and a lathe were present, while a metal-topped table held solvents and soldering equipment. The heavy atmosphere was full of the sour odour of heated metals. Brenner sniffed the air lovingly; he seemed to thrive on it. Then he turned to the long bench and, patting it, said: 'Put the case there, please. Now open it.'

McNally quickly unlocked and lifted the lid. Then he removed the piece of blanket that covered the contents of the case. The State Jewels of Lahkpore came sparkling into view. Brenner murmured something that sounded like an endearment under his breath, after which he screwed a jeweller's glass into his eye and stirred an index finger fastidiously amidst the loot, coming up with a diadem which he raised to the lense for his eager scrutiny. Then his agitated breathing bated, and the muscles of his gnarled hands became taut. An instant later he let out a soft curse and completed his exhalation, throwing the diadem from him disgustedly. His fingers scrabbled amidst the jewellery now, and this time he singled out a big claw-like ruby for his attention. The jewel, which had probably decorated the peak of the Maharajah's turban, looked worth a fortune in itself, but the old man cast it from him with a contemptuous 'pah'.

'What the hell are you doing?' McNally demanded, his anger blossoming out of the fear that seemed to be slowly distending his stomach. 'You don't chuck gems around like so much birdseed!'

'Gems!' Brenner brayed. 'Even birdseed is too good a name for them! Paste! Strass! Glass with a high proportion of oxide of lead! You've been done, my boy; fooled! The entire contents of your case are not worth your time and train-fare from Eastport!'

McNally's lips unloaded filth. He seized Brenner by the armpits of his waistcoat, shook him hard, then lifted the old man to the tips of his toes and glared into his face. 'Just how stupid do you imagine I am, you old fool?' he rasped. 'If you think I'm going to fall for that one, you've got another think coming. I'm not going to walk out of here with my tail between my legs and leave you a fortune. Not bloody likely, I'm not!'

'You're the fool, McNally!' Brenner

protested. 'I do honest business with my crooked friends. Let go of me, you young oaf! Pick the ruby up. Go on! Go on!'

McNally let go the old man, then hesitated. He could see truth behind the indignation that darkened Brenner's leaking eyes. Reaching across the bench, he picked up the ruby and passed it to his companion, who was impatiently snapping a finger and thumb. Then the jeweller opened a drawer beneath the bench and took out a large and powerful magnifying glass. 'Come here, McNally,' the old man said, 'and I'll show you the things a competent jewel thief should know.' He held the ruby up to the light and covered it with the magnifying glass, so that the curved layers of which the stone was composed became dimly visible. 'This ruby,' he went on, 'was built in a chemist's laboratory. Molten drops of chromium-aluminium oxide mixture have been fused in a flame of illuminating gas and oxygen. We in the trade call what comes out of this process *boule*. It can be cut, when cool, much as genuine stones are cut.'

'*Boule*, eh?' McNally growled. 'God help you, old man, if you're feeding me bull!'

'Here,' Brenner said resignedly, reaching out to his bench and picking up a damaged ring which contained a fair sized ruby. 'This is a genuine stone; pure carmine — from Burma. Look at it behind the magnifying glass. The layers that compromise it are flat, and there isn't a trace of an air-bubble. Now take another look at the synthetic stone. Are there not several traces of air-bubbles?'

'There are,' McNally admitted tersely.

'But you still don't believe,' the old man complained. 'Do you wish me to submit both stones to the cathode ray test?'

'What happens in that?'

'Synthetic stones, when exposed to cathode rays, go on glowing after the rays have been cut off. Genuine stones cease glowing in the same circumstances. I'll run the test if you wish.'

'Hell, no!' McNally exploded. 'I've had enough of this. I just don't dig why the Maharajah's agents went to the trouble and expense of having the Armoured Securities Express people transport a load of junk jewellery from London to Eastport.'

Brenner made a gesture of resignation. 'I see no point in it either, McNally. We can do no business because there's no business to do. I regret it as much as you do. But to me it's one more disappointment to put with the rest. Would you like a drink before you leave?'

McNally ignored the question. Teeth clenched, he reached out and retrieved the diadem, while Brenner threw the ruby back into the suitcase. 'There's got to be more to it,' McNally seethed, casting the diadem after the ruby. 'There's got to be!'

'That,' the old man said gravely, 'is between you and your belief. I wash my hands of it. Peace of mind is the important thing at my age.'

McNally opened his mouth to utter an impolite retort; but at that moment a door which overlooked the property's sunken backyard burst open and a big man wearing a Homburg hat and a crumpled raincoat entered the room.

Sudden fear made McNally want to vomit. 'You bastard!' he yelled. 'You've been listening at the door all the time! How in the devil's name did you get out there, Blessingay?'

10

McNally took a threatening step forward, but the chief inspector raised a staying hand and effectively covered the doorway. 'Sorry for this intrusion,' he said, his piggy little eyes grinning impenitently over the hairy, wrinkle-encrusted mounds at the tops of his cheeks. 'I'm so glad you know my name. It saves the trouble of introductions. I think your name is McNally?'

'You know damned well it is!' McNally seethed. 'You must have heard it once or twice while you were eaves-dropping.'

'Doing my duty,' Blessingay corrected. 'You're under arrest McNally.'

'What for?'

'Complicity in the murder of Eric Thomas Wilson, a guard in the employ of the Armoured Securities Express Company, and for taking part in armed robbery. We'll get to you in due course, Brenner. You're an old man. Old men don't run away.'

'It isn't fair!' Brenner bleated, trembling all over. 'I had nothing to do with any of it.'

'Tell that to the judge,' the chief inspector advised tersely. 'Pass me the case, please, McNally.'

With a deliberate thump from the heel of his hand, McNally closed and locked the lid of the suitcase. 'You can have it, Chief Inspector!' he exclaimed, leaping away from the bench and swinging at Blessingay's head with all his force. A corner of the case crunched through the big man's hat and sent him floundering against the wall, where he sank to one knee and shook his head dazedly.

McNally lunged through the now unguarded door. He found himself at the top of a flight of concrete steps. He scampered down them into the yard below. Green slime under the rain caused him to slip on the uneven flagstones. He peered about him as he caught his balance. On three sides blank brickwork faced him, but in the fourth wall he saw a gateway, and propelled himself towards it. The gate stood ajar. He jerked it open, passed through it, and cocked an ear across his shoulder as he heard lumbering footfalls on the steps behind him.

Pausing a split second to orient himself, McNally realized that he was standing on the far left of the recess that contained Brenner's shop. He ran directly on to the street, and made off to the left. Eyes screwed up against the driving rain, he pelted over the cobble-stones. A corner appeared on the left. He went round it, throwing a glance behind him at the same time. He saw Blessingay, paunch flopping and mouth agape, in full pursuit; but the man's age and bulk were against him, and it was obvious that he couldn't keep up his effort for long. McNally gave the chief inspector about two minutes to stay in the chase, and raced onwards confidently.

Then the lane which McNally was following narrowed as a high stone wall closed in on one side of it and an equally high line of iron railings appeared on the other. For a moment he thought the way was going to fizzle out altogether, but then he saw the mouth of an alley opening through the illusion of a dead end. He went into it, and his steps hammered on ancient paving-stones and built ringing echoes.

The alley soon came to an end. It issued into a railed off promenade that gave access to the walled cemetery of a medieval church, which was closely adjoined on either side by large buildings of the trade variety. McNally saw that what he had feared a minute ago had now happened. He had reached a dead end. He could enter the graveyard, yes; but stone walls at least nine feet high surrounded the unkempt acre of the burial place. Those walls, overhung as they were by dense yew foliage, were as totally confining as any about a prison exercise yard.

Slowing, McNally hesitated to enter the place. Then he heard Blessingay pounding through the narrows. Craning, he glimpsed the man emerging from the alley. McNally passed through the grave-yard gates. He had a rather vague idea of drawing the chief inspector after him, and then doubling back through the tomb-stones and passing out of the gate while his less agile pursuer was still trying to duplicate some of his earlier manoeuvres. But Blessingay was not to be deceived that easily. McNally saw the chief inspector stop plumb in the gateway, and hang forward, panting. Skidding to a halt beside a vault, McNally turned and stared at his follower, aware that he was going to speak and yet unsure of what to say. Finally, he gasped rather inanely: 'Get out of the road, you fat porpoise!'

'Pack this game up, McNally!' the chief inspector warned. 'You're penned in, and I don't want to hurt you!'

'You and whose army!' McNally jeered.

'Son, I've forgotten more about dirty fighting than you'll ever know,' came Blessingay's grim rejoinder. 'But suit yourself. Though I may as well tell you that I've no intention of standing here like numb chance and catching my death. I've got a police whistle in my pocket. A few blasts on it, and we'll have half the city constabulary coming to my aid. Do you want to make a big thing of it?'

McNally did not. No reason of personal sensitivity or better feeling came into it. Quite the contrary. He was desperate and wanted as few men about as possible. He meant to get out of this jam by any form of trickery or deception that was open to him. If necessary, he would certainly use further violence, though he knew he would have to go carefully about that. Blessingay might be a tub of lard, but he undoubtedly did know a lot when it came to the dirty stuff. The police were far from the lily whites the public believed them to be. Every manjack of them knew how to break bones and ruin the most important nerve centres. Blessingay would have to be caught off guard. The first blow must also be the last this time. He might as well start preparing the way for it; turn nice — smalmy even; get helpful — chat the old boy up.

McNally relaxed and started to grin. 'I suppose you're right, Chief Inspector. All this charging about does seem silly, doesn't it? I'm not going to push it. The chaps say you're the greatest. I'm ready to accept that now. How did you get on to me?'

'Birds of a feather, McNally,' Blessingay replied. 'You pick your women badly, and I have a lot of luck.'

'Gilda,' McNally said, more to himself than the man blocking his path. But how — ? He wanted to ask more questions; but he also didn't want to say too much. He thought hard. The Police must have called at Westmayne's home while the girl was there; he could see nothing else for it. That meant they had been summoned. By Westmayne? No, the man wouldn't have dared. Who, then? And to what precise purpose? Something had happened that he and Setters hadn't anticipated. It must have to do with the fake jewels which had come into the business; a new involvement centred about them, perhaps.

'Come here, McNally,' the chief inspector ordered.

McNally walked slowly towards the gate, the suitcase dragging from his right arm. He stopped obediently as the chief inspector raised a palm when about eight feet of ground separated them.

'Put the case down between us,' Blessingay said.

'You won't get much out of a load of paste,' McNally said cheerfully.

'I'll get enough,' came the retort. 'Don't get smart, son. Your best bet is to come clean.'

'Grass? You must be joking!' McNally stretched to the front and set the case down almost exactly between them. Then he lurched slightly, let out an 'ouch', and cupped his hands about his left ankle, massaging it vigorously. His upturned face wore a suitably pained expression.

'What's up?' Blessingay asked.

'I gave it a twist,' McNally lied. 'I skidded in something a dog left back there in the alley. I may need your shoulder to lean on.'

'My car isn't far away,' Blessingay said shortly, bending to pick up the case.

McNally jumped in. His right knee swept up viciously towards the chief inspector's jaw. But Blessingay, evidently prepared for the move, interposed a shoulder and jerked backwards, after which he straightened up and struck out with a braced forearm. The blow was a surprisingly powerful one. It struck McNally under the left armpit. He spun sideways and crashed into one of the pillars that formed the gateway to the burial ground. He rebounded into a tripping foot and a shoving hand. This time he fell with disastrous results, for the righthand side of his body struck the back of a seat which had been provided for visitors to the graveyard. He felt two or three of his ribs bend and crack, and agony lanced through him. Fury followed the pain, and, as he felt the chief inspector's fingers dig into his shoulders and wrench him up and round, he lashed out with every scrap of strength he possessed. The punch caught Blessingay on the point of the jaw. His eyes dilated, and his knees buckled. He fell on to his back and lay unconscious.

Holding his side and grimacing, McNally recovered the suitcase and ran out of the burial place. He re-entered the alley, passed through it at speed, and splashed along the lane beyond. Reaching the street again, he bore to the left and raced on for another fifty yards, coming to a bridge over the River Wensum. Brushing along the parapet, he raised his right arm in a bowling motion across his body and sent the suitcase arcing into space. A moment later he heard it splash down in the river beneath.

Unimpeded now, he cleared the old part of the city and moved into a district where the streets were wider and the buildings of a recent day. He tried to ignore the hurt he had received, but his ribs burned and throbbed. Before long, he found himself fighting for breath. But he knew he couldn't afford to ease up. Hard as he had hit Blessingay, he couldn't imagine the big copper staying down and out for any length of time. The chief inspector might already be conscious again and summoning the city police to the area. McNally rubbed the rain out of his eyes as he weighed up his situation. If he tried to stay in Norwich, he would certainly be caught before the afternoon was over. It was imperative that he make the most of his immediate freedom and anonymity. He must steal a car and get out of the city. His hope lay in the reaches of the county.

Then the frustration began. He saw no vehicles standing at the curbs, and the car parks were also empty. Again he was reminded that it was Sunday. Most of the motorists were at home. The few cars that he did see as his search progressed were parked in front of houses or other occupied buildings. Even he dare not attempt a theft which was too open and rash.

He dragged his weary legs up one street and down the next. His lungs seemed to be filling up with fire. A sense of desperation grew in him and exerted vice-like pressures on his brain. He experienced moments of confusion and disturbed orientation. He wondered how long it would be before policemen appeared from all directions and closed in upon him, whistles blowing and truncheons waving. His fear degenerated into illness, and his movements gradually lost all sense of purpose. He had reached the limit of his endurance.

Then he got a break. Entering another street, he saw on his right two large buildings with the name of a builder's merchant painted across their fronts. Between the buildings was the entrance to a yard; and standing well back in the opening was a blue Lancia. The car's design was tastefully simple, and he knew that it was capable of a fine performance. He gazed at it covetously, and hurried into the entrance, passing beyond the car to make sure that the yard was empty, and then returning to try the vehicle's door.

This opened without any trouble. Thrusting his head over the wheel, he saw that the key was in the ignition switch, so he slipped into the driver's seat, switched on and started up, then approached the road on a slipped clutch and prepared to swing out to the right; but just then a police car swept by from the other direction, and he had to slam on the brakes and bring the car to a jolting standstill. He saw the patrolman's frown, and thought for a moment that the officer was going to stop and tell him off; but the man was evidently too busy to make anything of the incident, for his vehicle swung unchecked around the next corner and disappeared.

Shaking with relief, McNally got the Lancia into motion again and surged off along the street. Rain blurred the windscreen before him, and he prodded about on the dash until he located the switch that brought the wipers into action. Peering out through an arc of washed-brightness, he made a right turn and followed a wide street up to some traffic lights; then, as the green came on, he passed over the junction, sped down a hill which took him past the old horse barracks, and eventually reached the approaches to a big round-about on the other side of the river. Here he swung into the outer traffic lane and turned towards the ring road, careful now to keep his speed at or around the limit for the area.

He reached the ring road a minute or two later. At this juncture he was faced with a real decision about which way to go. If he went to the left and out into the county, he would stand a good chance of getting away altogether; but his true desire was to turn to the right and head for Eastport, where a matter of vengeance required his attention. Yes, vengeance — for he believed that he had been made a mug of. His mind had been working slowly and deeply over the matter of the fake jewels, and he was now confident that he understood what had happened. Westmayne had been very clever indeed; but he wasn't going to get away with it.

McNally yanked his wheel to the right. Toe well down, he followed the ring road through extensive areas of new building. Then the long, outward curve of a steep hill checked him a little, and across open ground to the west he had a good view of the sombre buildings of Norwich Prison. In craning a bit during those moments of grim fascination, something else caught the corner of his eye. Far off, across the sprawling base of the hill, at the point where he had joined the ring road, a tiny blue light was flashing. It could only be the patrol car that he had seen earlier or another like it. He wondered if the Police had already received word about the stolen Lancia. It was possible, though not altogether likely. Still, he couldn't afford to take the smallest chance; so, as he saw the patrol car turn into the direction that he was himself heading, he pushed the accelerator to the floor and made for the main road which led to the coast.

Excitement gnawed at him savagely as he motored through Thorpe. He kept an eye on the mirror, but saw nothing of the police car as he left the outskirts of the city and a long stretch of almost straight road opened up behind him. All the same, his anxiety persisted. He knew the main highway to Eastport was well-patrolled, and decided to leave it as soon as possible and take to the by-roads. There was another reason why he made up his mind to do this; a physical one. The pain in his side had sapped him to a state of considerable weakness. He realized that he would never make it all the way back to the coast. He needed a long rest and a drink; and he knew a place where he could probably get both. It wasn't so far away either; not more than ten miles.

Slack's Hole, they called it. Few places were more remote. The owner of the land hired out his farmhouse to people looking for a day or two's peace and quiet. McNally had often taken Gilda there. Of course, there was the risk that the place would be already occupied, but he would have to take a chance on that.

A minute later, McNally slowed down and turned off into a narrow road on his right. The way cut diagonally across country, its general direction towards the sea. McNally passed between low hedges and flat, marshy fields, where the rain swirled eastwards as a fine mist and small herds of red poll cattle huddled under any fragments of shelter which were available. Travelling with reasonable care, he soon passed through a pair of small villages, used a narrow bridge to cross the Yare, and picked up a better road on the other side. Most of the time he felt on the edge of collapse, but he forced himself to keep going. Eventually he came to a cross-roads, where he turned back towards the river, travelled on for another half a mile, and then left the metalled way and entered a lane that ran between low banks. Rocking and jolting, he progressed slowly for a number of minutes, then came to a depression with a farmhouse and its out-buildings at the centre. Across the back of the hollow stretched the railway embankment, while the wall of a dyke bordered it on the right, and tussocky fields inclined shallowly towards the normal state of flatness on the left. There was mud everywhere, and water sloshed and gurgled under the wheels of the car as McNally turned through a gateway, pulled over to the left, and reversed across a corner of the farmyard into a dilapidated barn.

Switching off the engine, he sighed weakly and stepped out of the Lancia. He gazed towards the house and about as much of the property as he could see. He was in luck all right. There was nobody at home. Getting in would present no problem. At the far end of the house there was a window that wouldn't fasten properly. If you gave the frame a good shake, the catch came undone and you could thrust it upwards by the pressure of your palms against the glass. He had got in on one or two occasions like that, when he had mislaid his key.

He walked tiredly to the house, moved along its front, and turned the corner at its lower end, making for the window he had in mind. Reaching it, he did the things necessary to open it, and with the frame thrust upwards as far as it would go, was preparing to enter, when the roaring clatter of a passing diesel unit caused him to twist his face towards the railway line. He saw somebody looking at him from the guard's van, but paid no attention. Fatigue had drastically reduced his levels of fear and worry. His single wish was to get into the house and collapse on to a settee. If he could achieve that much, he would be well satisfied for the time being.

11

Consciousness wormed slowly out of the dust and cobwebs that enclosed Blessingay's brain. He couldn't bear the thought of opening his eyes. An upper phase of the subconscious kept warning him that a whole army of outraged nerve-ends were just waiting for the first glint of light on his retina to begin twisting and wriggling and writhing in the manner that would bring him most misery. He was ready to say it himself now. McNally was a rough handful. The chief inspector had never been hit so hard before in his life. But the blow had made one thing quite clear. McNally was violent; and he also wasn't to be trusted. There must be no further attempts to temporise with him. Next time they met, Blessingay would operate in terms of truncheon and handcuffs. The McNallys of this world couldn't be treated like human-beings.

The chief inspector raised himself into

a sitting position. He let his eyelids flicker and braved the influx of light. The revolt of his nerve-ends was even more agonizing than he had anticipated. Electric storms flared behind his temples, bombs roared, a couple of armoured divisions rumbled back and forth under his brainpan, and pattern after pattern of depth charges cracked and boomed. The suffering was so acute that he envied the dead in the earth nearby. He cursed his own good-nature, he cursed the policemen's lot, he cursed the day he had been born, and he cursed the rain that had soaked his back and the seat of his trousers.

Drawing his legs under him, he got shakily to his feet and reeled to the nearer of the gate pillars. Leaning against the stonework, he breathed deeply and rhythmically until the worst of the onslaught inside his head had expended itself. Then he had a look at his watch. The time was 4.15. He estimated that he had been unconscious for almost twenty minutes. McNally might be anywhere by now. Probably he had stolen a car and left the city. Anyway, it was too late to think in terms of blowing a whistle and starting a manhunt through the streets. Blessingay admitted to himself that he had fluffed an easy chance. Now he would have to think on a larger scale, plan more closely, and be prepared for a lot of work.

He left the graveyard, and trudged back to the café from which he had spent an hour or two watching Brenner's shop. Ignoring the curious glance of the bored proprietress, he ordered and quickly swallowed a cup of black coffee, then he left the building again and located the side-street in which he had parked his Citroen. Getting into the vehicle, he drove it into Tombland and stopped near the cathedral, where he went into a public call box and rang Eastport Police Station. 'It's the chief inspector here,' he told the operator on the Station switchboard. 'Put me through to Sergeant Logan.'

Logan came on the line a few seconds later. 'Hello, sir,' he said breezily. 'Having a nice time?'

'No, I am not,' Blessingay replied ferociously. 'What do you think I'm on, the work's outing? I suppose you've had your feet up most of the afternoon, and been flirting with the cat.'

'He's a tom, sir,' Logan remarked.

The chief inspector made a disdainful noise. 'It's McNally we want at the moment.'

'I rather thought it might be, sir.'

'Did you? Did you? Yes. The fact you found him away from home on a day like this must have seemed significant. We had it all wrong, you know. McNally turned up at Brenner's shop with a suitcase.'

'The Lahkpore jewels, sir?'

'Paste replicas,' Blessingay answered, a trace of sour superiority in his tones. 'I overheard some pretty dialogue at the back door, I can tell you. Can you see a young fellow like McNally being involved with the Sanderman woman? I can't. Nor can I see him as an expert housebreaker. He had help at Westmayne's place.'

'Yes, sir.'

'There's no doubt McNally was one of yesterday's hold-up gang,' the chief inspector went on. 'Whether the screws-man was or not, is another thing. I wouldn't think so. It looks to me like a matter of letting the loot get into the boss's keeping, then of lifting it off the boss.'

'Proving that against Westmayne is going to be quite a job, sir.'

'That's the reason why I want McNally,' Blessingay retorted irritably. 'Not to mention the fact that he busted me a beauty in the jaw when I had him cornered. McNally must be an extremely angry man. It looks to me as if a little trick of his back-fired badly. I'm speaking about the attempted robbery of Westmayne's safe in the Pleasure Land office. The Sanderman woman mentioned it at the right psychological moment, if you recall? I've no doubt that safe is a real tough one, and Westmayne planned to put the loot into it; but I feel equally sure that McNally and his pal pulled the fake Pleasure Land job to persuade the boss that the jewels would be more secure in Bellinger Place.'

'Only Westmayne's no fool,' Logan cut in. 'You think he saw through the ruse, and also how he could use it to his own advantage?'

'Precisely,' the chief inspector agreed. 'He hides the real jewels somewhere secure, puts the paste imitations in his safe, sits back and giggles while they're being stolen, and then tells the gang about the theft — adding, most probably, that he believes McNally is the culprit.'

'And the gang,' Logan continued, 'ardently directed by their boss, start hunting for McNally. If they catch him — '

'Or Westmayne catches him,' Blessingay interpolated.

'And don't kill him before he has a chance to talk, he'll only be able to tell them that he took a load of paste jewels to George Brenner's shop in Norwich. The fact that he did steal them from Westmayne's safe is going to predispose the gang to believe their boss when he says that the Maharajah of Lahkore's agents must have deceived everybody and sent only the paste replicas from London. But I don't think it will get that far.'

'Neither do I,' Blessingay remarked. 'To my mind, Westmayne is gambling that McNally will see through what's happened, come back to Eastport, and try to do him up good and properly as a matter of revenge.'

'Only Westmayne means to get in first,' Logan observed.

'And last,' Blessingay agreed flatly. 'We must catch McNally in the next few hours. I don't want him getting killed or seriously hurt. I can't see us pinning a lot on Westmayne and the gang — whoever they may be — without his testimony.'

'If he'll give it,' Logan muttered.

'We'll worry about that when we've got him!' the chief inspector retorted brusquely. 'I'm going up to the Norwich City Police Station now. I want to check on any car that was stolen here around four o'clock this afternoon. You'd better run a routine check on public transport. There's a slim chance McNally may try to box clever and come in that way. Can you manage to get hold of a photograph of him?'

Logan cleared his throat. 'That's already taken care of, sir.'

'How?' Blessingay asked suspiciously.

'I took a photo-copier into McNally's flat. There was a photograph of him with Gilda Kemp on his bedroom table.'

'Forget what I said about you being too honest to be a policeman,' the chief inspector advised dryly. 'All right, Sergeant. Let's cut the cackle. Circulate your photograph, and get to work.'

'Er, excuse me, sir,' Logan put in hurriedly.

'What?'

'Supposing McNally works everybody a real flanker and sits tight in Norwich or does a complete bunk?'

'He won't. The angry ones never do. Those whom the gods mean to destroy etc.' Blessingay made to return the receiver to its rest, then quickly put it back to his ear again. 'And no kid gloves. McNally has a sweet tongue, and a heart of flint. Don't listen to any of his kindly stuff, if you meet him, and don't be afraid to crack him one. Understand?'

'Perfectly, sir.'

The chief inspector lowered the receiver and weighed it in his hand. For a moment he felt inclined to toss it back on to the cradle in his best office manner. But in a sudden access of respect for G.P.O. property, he caught it between two hands and laid it down gently. Then he shouldered out of the telephone booth and returned to his car, drove on to Prince of Wales Road, cursed the one way system, and spent the next ten minutes describing an enormous half-circle which eventually brought him to the City Hall and the Police Station adjoining.

After leaving his car on the park opposite the City Hall, he entered the Police Headquarters, showed his warrant card to the sergeant at the desk, and asked if he could see the man at present in charge. A young constable led him deferentially into the presence of Superintendent Joe Shaner, one of Blessingay's best friends in the days of their youth. Shaner rose from behind his desk as the chief inspector entered his office and thrust out a hand. 'John!' he exclaimed delightedly. 'What a pleasant surprise!'

Blessingay met the other's grip, and they shook warmly. 'Nice to see you, sir,' he said, running an eye over the other's leonine head and very tall and wide-shouldered figure. 'You're looking fit.'

'Not so bad for an old 'un.'

'Not so old, sir. You don't look a day over forty.'

'Flatterer. We both know I shan't see fifty again.' Smiling, Shaner nodded dismissal to the lingering constable, who went out and shut the door. 'What's all this 'sir' business?'

'I fear you've out-run the old dog,' Blessingay answered wryly.

'They shoved me back into uniform in the process,' Shaner said regretfully.

'You always were a good administrator.'

'And you were always a good detective, John. Judge between the two, and decide who's gone ahead.' Shaner leaned forward, peering closely at the bruises on his visitor's jaw. 'What are you doing in Norwich, anyway?'

'Poaching.' Blessingay pointed wryly to the section of his face which had caught Shaner's interest. 'Serves me right, doesn't it?'

'And now you need our help?' the superintendent suggested with amusement.

Blessingay nodded. 'I'm blushing and hanging my head, sir.'

'You're as bad as ever!' Shaner declared.

'Pure gall,' Blessingay agreed resignedly. 'Barrels of it. What reports of stolen cars have you had in this afternoon? Anything around four o'clock?'

'I'll ask the Information Room,' Shaner said, flicking the switch on the intercom. A voice answered. The superintendent asked the questions put to him. There was silence for a few moments, then the voice provided the answers. 'Nothing much in the car line this afternoon, sir. Just one pinched — at 16.10 — from a building wholesaler's yard in Frog Street. A blue Lancia, 1963, registration number J.B.K. 189. The owner ran out of his office nearby when he heard the car being driven away. He phoned us up within minutes. We had a patrol car in the area, but our driver had no luck. All county patrols have since been issued with the registration number and description of the stolen vehicle, sir.'

'That's all you've got?' Shaner queried.

'That's all, sir.'

Shaner switched off the intercom.

'There you are, John. Have we helped?'

'Yes,' Blessingay said. 'Where is Frog Street, sir?'

'Want to go into the map room?'

'No. Roughly, I mean.'

'To the right of the old M. at G.N. railway station.'

Blessingay's brow corrugated thoughtfully, then he gave a slow, satisfied nod. 'Yes, I'll settle for that,' he said. 'About the right time and place. I'll act on it.' He paused, blowing on to a palm that he held near his mouth. 'Let's see. We have a chap, a pretty desperate one, who wants to leave the city and return to Eastport. For obvious reasons, he would wish to avoid the centre of Norwich, so he'd use the outer streets — '

'And the ring road,' Shaner put in, answering the prompting note in his visitor's voice. He'd probably go up through Plumstead and down through Thorpe. But would he stick to the main road after that?'

'That's what I'm wondering,' Blessingay said. No, I don't think he would. He'd turn off on to the country roads at

222

the first opportunity. Postwick?'

'Postwick,' the superintendent confirmed. 'John, you've got me curious. What particular case is this?'

'Our beauty.'

'The Lahkpore jewels? I thought it might be. A barbarous lot you've got on the coast. I've been meaning to pay you a visit, John, but I haven't been able to get my missionary's licence through.'

'Oh, we're fairly civilized in Eastport, sir,' Blessingay said with a straight face. 'Except on Saturday nights, that is. Of course, our yobs do still eat missionaries and use their bones for crochet hooks — and they're not too particular about policemen — but if you were to slip in quietly, disguised as a thorough-paced villain, you might get out again unscathed. Mind, I'm not promising anything.'

'I'll tell my wife John Blessingay has settled among the headhunters.'

'She'll almost certainly be convinced that I'm their chief,' Blessingay observed wryly.

'Ann, I must admit, was never one of your fans.'

'I have that effect on women,' the chief inspector admitted. 'May I use your phone, sir.'

'Help yourself.'

Blessingay went to the superintendent's desk and picked up the telephone. He dialled the number of the Eastport Police again, and asked if Sergeant Logan was in the Station. 'I think he's just come in, sir,' came the reply from the desk. 'I'll just ring around the building and see. Hold on, please.'

'Right,' Blessingay said, tapping a fingernail on the edge of the desk as he waited, and about a minute later he again heard the sergeant's voice in his ear. 'Hello, Logan. I've got something for you.'

'And I for you, sir,' Logan countered, sounding rather excited.

'Very well. Let's have your sixpenny-worth first.'

'We struck oil with public transport, sir.'

'You did what?' Blessingay demanded, grinning through his scowl as he glanced at Shaner.

224

'I went to the railway station myself, sir. A guard by the name of Hector Isles was fresh in from Norwich. He took one look at McNally's mugshot and told me that he'd had a barney with the chap on Thorpe Station. But that's not it. He actually saw McNally again, in rather odd circumstances, while on the return journey to Eastport. He was at the window of his guard's van, and saw our suspect breaking into a farmhouse at a place called Slack's Hole. Isles was — '

'Where on earth is that?' the chief inspector broke in sharply.

'The guard told me, and I've also had a look on the map, sir. It's not far from Reedham. The farmhouse stands at the bottom of a lane. It's a dead end. I've called two cars in, and raked up six Bobbies. Okay, sir?'

'You know damned well it is. McNally is probably planning to hole up until tonight. But if he should pull out before you get to Slack's Hole, look for a blue Lancia J.B.K. 189. The county patrols already have the registration number and description of the vehicle. Any questions?'

'No, sir.'

'I'll get out to Slack's Hole as quickly as possible. I hope to see you there. Good luck.'

' 'Bye, sir.'

Blessingay hung up as he heard the receiver at the other end of the line click back to rest.

'Good news?' Shaner asked.

'I think we've got our man where we want him,' the chief inspector replied. 'We've had a bit of luck; but that sergeant of mine is a good boy.'

'Logan, isn't it?'

'Yes.'

'I thought we were going to get him as an inspector a while back, but the selection board decided that he was still a bit young for the appointment.'

'Young, be damned!' Blessingay scorned. 'I wish I'd been half as good when I was his age. He deserves to get on; and he will. But I mean to hang on to him as long as I can.'

Shaner nodded his understanding. 'The first class ones are few and far between.'

Blessingay glanced at the floor a

moment, then thrust out his hand. 'Well, goodbye, sir, and thanks a lot for your help.'

'Don't mention it, John,' Shaner said, shaking hands firmly. 'I hope it won't be long before we meet again.'

'We'll have to have a day out together,' Blessingay agreed, as they walked towards the office door, 'and drink a pub dry. Don't bother to leave your work. I can see myself out.'

They parted at the door, and Blessingay hurried out of the Police Station and crossed the road to reach the car park. Getting into his vehicle, he manoeuvred it off the park as swiftly as possible; then, muttering about the one way system for a second time, he found his way out of the city and headed eastwards at high speed.

12

After resting for ten minutes on the settee in the farmhouse living-room, McNally felt sufficiently restored to get up and shamble to the liquor cupboard in the adjoining room. Aside from the pleasant and helpful qualities of alcohol, he needed its numbing powers to suppress the incessant throbbing of his damaged ribs. If he could once get relief from the pain, he would soon overcome his fatigue.

He tried the cupboard, but found it was locked. Anger swept through him. He knew what he wanted, and meant to have it. Picking up the poker from the hearth, he rammed it into the gap at the bottom of the cupboard and applied sufficient leverage to split the wood and burst the lock. Gasping from the effort, he tossed the poker back into the hearth and peered into the cupboard, finding an empty gin flask, a Martini bottle with about a mouthful in it, and a bottle of Vodka that was three parts full. He had no liking for Vodka; it was tasteless muck in his opinion; but this looked like the real stuff — smuggled in from Estonia. It's proofage wasn't marked; but it was certainly strong enough to anaesthetize a man's hurts or knock a horse over.

Digging a dusty tumbler out of the sideboard, McNally uncorked the bottle and splashed a good drink into the bottom of his glass. He drank it down. gagging as the raw spirit burned his throat and stomach. Then he stepped back into the living-room, carrying the bottle and glass with him, and stretched out on the settee again. He poured himself another drink, and for several minutes sipped and dozed, his thoughts gaining a new clarity as the soporific effects of the alcohol gathered in his ribs. Slowly, he let go. He was safe here. He couldn't imagine anybody searching for him in Slack's Hole in a thousand years. Looked at reasonably, the alert for him must be county-wide by this time. He would stand little or no chance of entering Eastport unobserved by the

Police in daylight. But after dark, the tale might be a different one; anyway, his chances would be at least ten times as good. He could wait. His first flush of malice had receded; and he really needed time to consider exactly what he would do to Westmayne when they were alone together.

The idea that the gang-boss might be prepared for his coming passed through McNally's mind, but it didn't bother him very much. He had every confidence that he would come out on top in a clash between Westmayne and himself. He had the beating of his ex-boss on every level. Not that he didn't admire the adroitness of Westmayne's double-shuffle with the paste replicas of the Lahkpore jewels; the trick had been clever enough; but it had also been smart-Alecky and lacked adequate safety mechanisms. Its complacency showed a disdain for the man it had been set to outwit, and that angered McNally most of all. Gilda's defection to a man who might have greater masculine charm, he could take; not easily, and not in the belief that it truly was so — but he could take it. Sex was sex; people liked a change. But chicanery was chicanery. Westmayne ought to have shown more style. He also ought to have fired that bitch of a housekeeper of his before switching his affections to Gilda. That woman wanted her neck wrung! It could only have been she, no doubt inspired by jealousy, who had brought the Police into the business and complicated it to a point of disaster for everybody concerned. McNally's mind wandered on. All kinds of half-related resentments sprang up against Westmayne now, and he realized that he was getting slightly drunk. Even a man of his capacity couldn't swill neat Vodka indefinitely. He would have to lay off the bottle. It had served its purpose. His ribs hardly hurt him at all now, and he felt much more like himself.

Even so, he poured out a final drink and took a good sip at it before stretching out an arm and placing it on the table behind the settee. Then, linking his hands behind his head, he listened drowsily to the silence, half aware that something sensed rather than heard had brought the back of his mind to alertness. Suddenly the faintest sound reached him from the kitchen on his left. His ears strained hard, and quick-forming tension drove a lump into his throat. He heard the lightest of footfalls and a soft brush of clothing. Had he imagined it? No, there it was again. Moving very quietly, he put his feet to the carpet and straightened up; then he took two rapid steps to the kitchen door, which was standing ajar. There was somebody in the house all right. He could feel a fresh draught pushing stale air into his face. There must be a window open.

He doubled a fist, and waited. The kitchen door moved an inch or two. McNally braced himself, but his reactions were too slow to counter the sudden appearance of Westmayne through the door; and, as he tried to make up for his tardiness, the muzzle of an automatic thrust into his face and struck him between the eyes, knocking him backwards. Shock and fury exploded through him as he recovered his balance, and the impulse to hit out and damn the consequence was almost more than he could resist; but he realized that West-mayne had come to kill him, and that if he wanted to stay alive a little longer, he must behave himself. While life remained, so did hope; that was another true saying. 'Well, look who's here!' he jeered. 'If it isn't old mastermind himself!'

'You fancy your weight, don't you, McNally?' Westmayne grated. 'But your cleverness is secondhand stuff. The old safe dodge has been used a time or two, you know.'

'Now he tells me!'

Westmayne's eyes narrowed. 'You're drunk, McNally, and that's how you're going to leave this world!'

'Here comes a candle to light you to bed — !' McNally laughed savagely. 'Give Gilda my love, and tell her I hope she rots!'

'She's a smart girl. She knows which side her bread is buttered on.'

'So it seems. You'd never have found me here if she hadn't told you about this place.'

'Yes. She thought you'd hide up here until after dark.'

'You two will run out of brains if you use them so hard. My word! You must have been bloody confident! But I'll tell you this. If I hadn't hurt myself, I probably wouldn't have come here, and that would've upset all your calculations, wouldn't it?'

'You're here.'

'To my cost. Never trust a woman.'

'Don't be too sad.'

'When did she start doing me dirt?'

'Mind your own business!'

'That's what I'm trying to do.'

'Your troubles will soon be over,' Westmayne mocked. 'You're an extravagant thinker, McNally, and an extravagant thinker becomes an extravagant talker. You told her too much during your cuddlesome frolics together. It was your big ideas that set Gilda thinking — and then me. She is a clever girl, that one, McNally. You planned to do too much with your share of the loot. In your mind, you were already splashing it around like a millionaire. The twenty thousand quid you were likely to have picked up after expenses wouldn't have gone that far. It certainly isn't a sum on which a man can promise an expensive woman a lifetime of luxury.'

'True,' McNally conceded. 'You and Gilda should do much better on the arrangement you've since made for yourselves.'

'The arrangement *you* made for us,' Westmayne retorted.

'I suppose I put that idea into your heads, at that,' McNally admitted. 'Fool-like, I made the whole thing possible. Oh, you innocent darlings!' He smiled tightly, and unclenched his hands, looking at the palms. 'I suppose you'll show my corpse to the boys?'

'Naturally they'll want to see the remains of the rat who pinched their loot. I'll see you get a good funeral. I'll bury you about two miles off shore, with iron bars at your head and feet.'

'Sounds comfortable.'

'Wait till the mackerel get at you!'

'What are the boys going to think when you disappear with Gilda?'

Westmayne laughed unpleasantly. 'That's right, McNally, keep me talking. There'll be enough police activity in Eastport before long to give me a good excuse for disbanding. The lads, worthy as they are in their respective ways, are petty crooks at heart. They'll soon forget about me once I'm no longer there to provide them with jobs and a living. News from the flash sets in foreign places isn't in their line. They move in the wrong circles.'

'You've got it all worked out,' McNally admitted. 'You might get away with it. But how much do the coppers know at this minute?'

'Without you to croak, how much can they prove?'

'That's another good point.'

'I haven't missed a thing,' Westmayne said, his face hardening as he made a small but significant adjustment to the manner in which he held his gun. 'Stand back in front of the fireplace. On the carpet.'

'My shroud?' McNally asked, trying to keep his voice steady as he obeyed.

'How did you guess?' Westmayne inquired. 'Stand up straight.'

McNally drew a deep breath and stood

up as straight as he could. His brain was racing, but he could see no way out of this spot. Perhaps he wasn't so clever after all. What a pity he had to find out so late. He watched the automatic rise and cover his heart. Then Westmayne started pressing the trigger, but a train went rattling by on the tracks nearby, and for a split second the gang boss's attention wavered.

Slim though the chance was, McNally seized it. He jumped to the right as Westmayne's gun roared, The bullet burned through the sleeve of McNally's raincoat, missing his left arm, and he swept the tumbler off the table and flung its contents into Westmayne's face. The gang-boss sent a hand clawing to his eyes as the Vodka burned and stung. He fired again, but this time blindly. Ducking under the weapon, McNally screwed across the fireplace and seized the poker from the hearth. He let go a back-handed swipe at Westmayne's gun-wrist. The gang-boss shrieked in agony, and the automatic leapt from his grasp and landed on the settee. Instinctively, he made a grab with his left hand to recover it, but before his fingers could touch the butt, reason blacked out in his assailant's mind. McNally slashed the poker across Westmayne's shoulders, and, as the gang-boss floundered forward, raised it again and brought it down with all his force across the base of his enemy's skull. He heard bone pop and crunch, and Westmayne dropped flat on his face and lay still. Blood splashed blackly out of his nose and ears.

McNally bent over the prostrate form. He felt dizzy and short of breath. Some minutes passed before his brain and eyes cleared. Then he tossed the poker into a corner, knelt beside Westmayne, and turned the man on to his back. The gang-boss's clenched teeth showed whitely, and unspeakable horror had frozen into his sightless eyes. McNally felt for a pulse, but the gesture was only a formality. Westmayne was dead.

Rising to his feet, McNally reeled to the table and grabbed the bottle of Vodka. He put it to his lips and took a long pull at the raw spirit. Soon he began to cough, and pain flashed up and down his right side. Pitching the bottle from him, he watched it land on the floor and roll, splashing spirit as it vanished under a chair. Then he turned and stirred the corpse with his toe. He was a murderer. Westmayne had been right. He had had it in him to kill. The gang-boss had paid with his life for being right.

Sinking down on to the settee, McNally considered what to do for the best. Before long he remembered that, at the back of the house, there was an old well. It was boarded up, and had been for some time, but he could soon attend to that. Westmayne's body could go into the well, and the planks be restored. That way the killing might go undiscovered for years. There was one small difficulty. The man must have left a car somewhere in the vicinity. But if McNally found this and drove it away himself, to abandon at some point far distant, the presence of the Lancia in the barn would tell the Police only that their wanted man had been in Slack's Hole. Only Gilda would be in a position to suggest what could have happened to Westmayne, but she would be unlikely to risk a move like that — even if McNally let her live long enough to make it!

He rubbed a knee as he kept his thoughts moving. He still meant to have the Lahkpore jewels. Gilda must know where they were. Before he did anything final to her lovely neck, he would persuade her to show him the hiding place. Then he became aware of Westmayne's gun lying beside him on the settee. Why not? Principles were gone; all barriers were down. He picked the weapon up and shoved it into his pocket. There was nothing like a gun to scare a woman half to death. Everything was decided, then. So be it. His cause was by no means lost. In fact, things might be coming good again.

Rising, he walked through into the kitchen. The window above the sink was open. At one corner of the sill lay the screwdriver which Westmayne had used to slip the catch. Climbing into the sink, McNally backed awkwardly through the window and lowered himself down the outer wall to the ground. Then he walked away from the house, rounded a clump of crab-apple trees, and came to the steeple-shaped wooden structure that covered the top of the well. He studied the several bars of wood that had been nailed over the well door, and came to the conclusion that he could pull them off with his hands. The strips were grey and weather-aged, A few bangs with a brick would soon restore them to their places once Westmayne's body had been dropped out of sight.

Turning from the well, McNally took a couple of steps towards the house and stopped in his tracks. His heart missed a beat as he tipped an ear towards the lane. His apprehension mounted as the seconds passed. He could hear cars approaching the farm. He tried to persuade himself that the vehicles were going to turn off somewhere, but he knew this was absurd; the lane had no branches. Then, through the gap between the end of the house and the barn, he saw the first car coming into view. It was the type of vehicle which he had most feared to see: a police patrol car. Spinning round, he leapt back into the cover of the wall and crouched, with one eye peering over the top. He saw the patrol car swing on to the property through the farmyard gate; then a similar vehicle followed it, and both halted about a dozen yards away from the house. The engines stopped, and constables began to scramble out, while a young man in plain clothes shouted instructions from a front seat in the first car to appear. The operation looked extremely efficient and formidable.

Realizing that the farmhouse was about to be surrounded, and that his present hiding place must soon be discovered, McNally crabbed towards a hedge behind him that marked the boundary of the garden. He was careful to keep the trees between himself and the building, though the cover which the growth afforded rapidly decreased as the line of observation lengthened between his movements and the corner of the house. He saw a constable trotting along the lower end of the building, and was afraid that he must be seen; but an instant later he spotted a ditch running along the base of the hedge, and scrambled down into it, swearing to himself as cold and muddy water drenched him to the knees and soaked his sleeves as he bent forward into it and began wading along the channel in the direction of the barn.

'McNally!' he heard a voice shout. 'We know you're in there, so come on out! The building is surrounded! you can't get away!' There was a long, echoing pause; then the voice added: 'Do you hear, McNally?'

He could hear well enough. Let the young chap bawl all he liked. While he was doing that, he and his men were doing nothing else. McNally used every second gained to full advantage.

'Very well, McNally!' the voice went on. 'We're coming in after you! Now be warned! If you've got a grain of sense, you won't resist arrest! We shan't be gentle if you behave foolishly!'

He'd bet on that. Not after what he'd done to old Blessingay. They'd pay him back tenfold if they got the chance. But he didn't intend to give them the chance.

By the time they had realized the significance of the open kitchen window, he would have done something very positive about escaping from the farm.

He waded into a deeper part of the ditch, moving faster now. A simple question filled his mind. How had the Police found out that he was hiding in Slack's Hole? Had they, perhaps, put a tail on Westmayne? No. After all, it had been his own name, McNally, that had been called just now. Was it possible, then, that Gilda, with a view to making a clear field for herself, had set the coppers after the gang-boss? No again, and for the same reason as last time. He was baffled. But he mustn't let it disturb him; he was going to need all his concentration soon.

McNally reached a point where the rear wall of the barn covered the ditch. He dragged himself towards the far end of the building. Between slips and splashes, he was now almost completely soaked to the skin. Grimacing in his discomfort, he came to a spot near the corner of the barn where the bank angled back steeply from the channel. Here he scrambled out of the water and hauled himself on to the bank above, crouching in the shelter of tarred clay lumps as he squeezed muddy liquid out of his turn-ups.

Then he crept along the side of the barn until he reached its front corner, where he peeped out across the farmyard to discover how the Police were now positioned. He got the impression that most of them had gone into the farmhouse, though two remained outside and were now standing at either end of the building so that they would have a good view if anybody should jump out of a window and make a break for it. The nearer man was not more than thirty feet away, much too close to risk any but the most stealthy movements behind his back. McNally thought he could reach the Lancia and get into it without being detected, but he had doubts as to whether he could start up and get away before the constable got near enough to use physical violence. Nevertheless, the danger would have to be accepted. McNally knew that this was the only chance he was likely to get. At any moment now the men in the house were going to realize that he had already left the building and transfer their search outside. He might manage to handle one policeman, but he wouldn't have a hope against a half a dozen of them.

Inching round the corner, he entered the barn, his eyes never leaving the constable's back. Tip-toeing swiftly, he reached the Lancia and knelt beside it, his fingers twisting at the doorhandle. The door opened with a faint click, and, with his torso cramped forward, he slipped into the driving seat and pressed the starter.

The engine clattered and whirred, and threatened to die; but it picked up and roared into full life as McNally pumped the accelerator. He slammed the door, slipping into gear, shot out of the barn, and went splashing and lurching towards the gate. From the corner of his eye, he saw the policeman spin round, gape a moment, and then give chase, determined to cut him off before he could swing into the lane. McNally spun the wheel sharply, slewed over to the left, and presented only an acutely angled boot to the officer as he passed through the gateway. But the policeman saw through the move, and dived round the rear of the car, coming up on its off side as the bonnet straightened into the middle of the track. Truncheon out, the man threw himself across the cowling and hung on grimly. McNally pushed his foot to the boards, and went weaving all over the lane, bumping and bouncing through the pot-holes with such violence that it was a miracle the machine hung together. Through it all, the policeman managed to keep his grip on the bonnet, and finally he succeeded in steadying himself long enough to strike the windscreen a truncheon-blow that reduced it to a thousand starry cracks.

McNally trod on the brakes as his vision disappeared. The car almost stood on its bumper. He had a vague impression of the constable spinning over the nose of the vehicle and vanishing towards the ground. Opening his door, McNally lunged out of the Lancia and rounded the bonnet, where he saw the officer, helmet askew and a dazed look in his eyes, trying to pull himself up the radiator grill. Without more ado, McNally pulled the automatic from his pocket and laid the barrel across the man's nape, causing him to collapse instantly. Screwing a hand into the constable's collar, McNally dragged him away from the car and dumped him at the side of the lane, after which he hurried back to the door of the Lancia and saw one of the police cars emerging from the farmyard which was still no more than three hundred yards to the rear. In sheer desperation, McNally raised the automatic and blazed off four shots at the vehicle. One or more of them must have hit the mark, for the patrol car stopped momentarily and only moved off again at the slowest pace. Meantime, McNally got back into the Lancia, smashed the windscreen out with a slashing movement of his gun barrel, and set the vehicle back into motion again.

Wind and rain blew in upon him as he picked up speed. The rear vision mirror blurred, but it showed him that the police car had now entered the chase in earnest. Disregarding both himself and the vehicle, he drove at the kind of reckless pace which again set the bodywork quivering violently and the springs pinging away in agony. Up and down behind the wheel he bounced, his left knee banging against the edge of the cut-back dashboard and his cracked ribs playing him up cruelly. He bit his lower lip until the blood ran, and cold sweat dribbled between his eyes. But the mirror showed him that he was gaining ground; a lot of it. The police car was now little more than a toy image in the depths of the glass. If he could reach the open road with a quarter of a mile lead over his pursuers, he would soon out-distance and lose them in the wide stretch of country that lay between him and the coast.

But this was not to be. As he bucketed into a lefthand bend, a car came speeding at him from the other direction. The driver of the machine braked and slewed over to his off side. McNally could see there was no way through, but his fierce compulsion to go on made him accelerate. He yanked the Lancia over to the right and forced its near side wheels up the bank, then went clawing and spinning towards the inadequate gap along the other vehicle's canting side. The Lancia started to slide. McNally fought it over to the right harder than ever; but the greater the effort, the more he lost traction and broadsided towards the second car. There was a crash, a momentary lurching, and a heave; then the Lancia's engine cut out, and it shuddered to a standstill, locked door to door with the vehicle opposite, which was half in and half out of the ditch.

McNally burst out of his car, waving his gun. He glared ferociously at the other driver, and recognized the man as Blessingay. He made a rude gesture with two fingers, then, as the chief inspector carefully abandoned his car and slipped into the ditch, he scrambled over the bank on his right and set off across the fields at a run. If the Police wished to catch Dave McNally, they would have to go all the way. And he meant *all* the way.

13

Climbing out of the ditch, Blessingay stamped shoes that slopped with water, set his hands on his hips, thrust out his jaw, and glared after the fleeing McNally. Then he turned his head and scowled to his right as the patrol car which had been chasing the Lancia stopped a few yards away. He watched Logan jump out of the car, and stared at the younger man accusingly; then he stabbed a finger after the fugitive and bellowed. 'Get after him, damn it! Don't stand there like a stuffed dummy!'

The chief inspector suited his own actions to his words. He crossed the lane in two lumbering strides and scrambled over the bank. Then he set off across the field at a remarkable pace for one who had been through so much that day. Logan surged by him a moment later, and he heard the constables on his heels. He urged everybody onwards with a sweeping movement of his right arm. The chase was no means hopeless. McNally had a lead of about two hundred yards, but he didn't appear to be going well. In fact he had started losing ground fairly obviously. They were going to catch the young son-of-a-gun. It would soon be all over.

Blessingay summoned up his will to keep going. Then he heard Logan shout: 'He's got a pistol, sir, and he's already used it!'

'I can't help about that!' the chief inspector barked. But he did care; he cared a lot. He hated exposing unarmed constables to the mercies of a desperate thug with a gun. But there was no escaping duty; it had to be done. Every man present knew that.

He ran on as hard as he knew how. Somehow he managed to keep in front of most of his younger and far more athletic subordinates. Chest burning and ripples and flashes of vertigo passing through his sight, he drove the party to the limit. The fugitive's lead had been cut by half. There was definitely something wrong with McNally. He suspected that the crook was hurt about the body. But so much the better, he thought grimly; so much the better.

Then Blessingay saw McNally crane round. The young man's face was a grey oval in the murk. McNally stumbled, and then he stopped, turning towards his pursuers on braced legs. Light gleamed dully on the automatic which he extended in his right hand. The weapon flashed and barked several times in quick succession. Blessingay ducked his head involuntarily and checked his stride. Then one of the constables near him let out a cry, stumbled, and collapsed on his knees. Halting now, the chief inspector turned and ran over to the man, waving for Logan and the remainder of the uniformed men to continue the chase; for McNally had ceased firing and resumed his flight.

'All right, lad?' Blessingay asked, as he knelt beside the wounded officer.

'Yes, sir,' the other gasped, his mouth wrenched by pain.

'Good chap,' the chief inspector said.

'You carry on, sir,' the constable insisted, his thin, almost ascetic features attempting to grin. 'I'll be all right.'

'I'm sure you will,' Blessingay agreed. 'It's your shoulder, isn't it? Wad a handkerchief under your tunic. We'll come back for you in a minute.'

'Thank you, sir.'

I deserve some thanks, Blessingay thought bitterly, as he thrust himself erect and moved off after the receding figures of the policemen. McNally was more than a hundred yards in advance of his men again. The fugitive was nearing a stile set in a tall hedge. He saw McNally clamber over it, and vanish to the left. Logan put in a spurt. Blessingay silently applauded the sergeant's superb fitness. If Logan had made a mistake in Slack's Hole, he was certainly trying his hardest to make up for it now. Splendid — so long as he didn't get a bullet for his reward.

Then the sound of a car starting up came from the other side of the hedge. Startled, the chief inspector broke stride. Surely not that! The gods couldn't be that unkind! He forced his aching legs back into a full run, and in less than a minute he had reached the stile, climbed it, and joined the constables who were standing on the other side. Anger swept through him as he saw the frustration on the flushed young faces. Unreasonably, he wanted to give them a piece of his mind, but he got control of himself and began walking in slow circles as he gazed along the lane to where Logan was standing under a tree and staring helplessly at the blue exhaust fumes which were thinning away over a T junction about fifty yards beyond him. 'All right, Logan!' he finally called. 'You'd better come here!'

The sergeant turned, and trotted back to the stile. He looked crestfallen. 'Sorry, sir,' he said.

'Some mothers have 'em,' Blessingay agreed frostily. 'Whose car did he get away in?'

'I think it must have been Westmayne's, sir. The luck just wasn't with us. I didn't catch more than a glimpse of it. It's a coffee colour, I believe; but I couldn't give the make or number.'

The chief inspector scowled. 'Westmayne's?'

'He's dead, sir.'

'By jove!'

'He's lying in the farmhouse down in Slack's Hole. The back of his head has been smashed in.'

'McNally?'

'I don't see who else.'

'No wonder he's using a gun.'

'I should imagine it was Westmayne's, sir.'

'You think McNally may have been defending himself?'

Logan nodded. 'But making too good a job of it.'

'Much too good. What went wrong down at the farmhouse?'

'McNally was already out of the house when we got to it, sir, but we'd no means of knowing that. I saw the Lancia in the barn, and deployed the men, as I thought, to cover all eventualities. But McNally is a slippery one.'

Blessingay fingered his jaw wryly; his anger was on the ebb. 'I know that. What about the farm? Who owns it?'

'I asked Information to do a bit of digging, sir. They radioed what they'd found out while we were on the way here.

The farm is owned by a chap named Moncrief. He does just enough with the land to keep him out of trouble with the Ministry. He lets the farmhouse out to people wanting a little peace and quiet. No questions asked. In other words, it's a kind of rural pad with its quota of dirty weekenders.'

'The girl,' Blessingay muttered. 'The sins that you do by two and two — '

'You must pay for one by one,' Logan completed. 'Yes, sir, it was probably Gilda Kemp who put Westmayne on to McNally. It could go hard with her.'

'Assuming we're right, yes,' Blessingay agreed, turning purposefully on his heel. 'Jutland Street was the address Gilda Kemp gave, wasn't it?'

'The flats — yes, sir.'

Blessingay heaved his toad-like bulk over the stile and indicated that everybody was to follow him.

'I think we should cover Bellinger Place, too, sir,' Logan said, hurrying to catch up as they retraced their steps across the field. 'A man on each place.'

'Yes, yes,' the chief inspector agreed.

'We'll radio the Station as soon as we get back to the patrol car. That ought to take care of our worry over Gilda Kemp. This case gets more interesting as it goes along.'

'New possibilities opening up all the time.'

'That's what worries me most, Sergeant,' Blessingay said. 'I keep getting little buzzes.'

'Buzzes, sir?' Logan asked politely.

'From a mind alien to my previous bump of things. I expect that sounds like a lot of rot to you, but there's always something we don't understand at work in that direction. I saw a pattern form, but there were small things wrong with it; so I pulled that pattern up and found another and more complex one beneath it. Now I can see something wrong with the second and I've started pulling that up too. Beneath it is a third pattern. I'm not sure about it yet, but I believe it's the truth. I hope my grip holds, Logan. I don't want anybody else killed, but I'm afraid there's going to be more business for the mortuary yet.'

'I hope you're wrong, sir,' Logan said, as the patrol car and the crashed vehicles came fully into view again.

'So do I, young man,' Blessingay said — 'so do I.'

14

McNally could hardly believe his luck as he drove along in the Viva. He had been running blindly and was just about ready to fold up when he had come upon the car. Westmayne had certainly left it in a well-hidden and unlikely spot before setting out for Slack's Hole across the fields. The gang-boss could never have dreamed it possible that the vehicle would give such vital aid to the man he had set out to kill.

Still keeping to the minor roads, McNally drove as fast as was consistent with safety. Pain racked him, but compared with what his fate might have been, he welcomed the pangs; they told him he was still very much alive. But he felt the need to get away from these great open spaces. The endless fields and marshlands made him feel naked and exposed. The sooner he entered Eastport, the better he would like it. He needed the presence of many walls about him again. His psyche yearned for their security and enclosing secrecy. He was no country-man; he despised the land and the poetry of the seasons.

Slowing at a sharp corner, he changed gear and moved into a short but sudden incline. His mind flashed out towards Gilda like a whiplash, then curled back negatively in its immediate spatial frustra-tion. He wondered how long it would take the Police to clear the lane that led into Slack's Hole and get their patrol cars through. Some little while, he guessed, but it was the use to which they would put their radio that really bothered him. The coppers must be fully aware that Gilda had been his mistress, and the more seamy facts about Slack's Hole wouldn't be hard to find out. An astute brain like Blessingay's would soon guess that Gilda must have primed Westmayne to the possibility of finding him at the farm-house, and McNally saw that the chief inspector would automatically assume that he was now heading for the girl. That meant they would give her Police protection whether she wanted it or not — and if his increasingly big suspicions were correct, their protection would be the last thing she would wish for.

Again he was forced to concentrate on his driving. At the other side of the small hill, he turned another corner and entered the approaches to a larger one. He dropped into third gear again, and began to climb. He was almost half way up the hill when a green Morris Oxford came round the corner at the top and began descending towards him. He peered at the driver and occupants of the vehicle for a moment without comprehending who they were; but then he recognized Fred Golson, Bill Piper, and Ritchie Fairclough, the men with whom he and Westmayne had pulled the Armoured Securities Express job. Fred Golson, who was at the wheel of the Morris, saw him in the same moment of recognition, and shouted something to his companions, then began steering an interception course.

Mindlessly almost, McNally pulled the automatic from his pocket, thrust it out of the window beside him, and fired at Golson as fast as he could press the trigger. The windscreen of the Morris became a ruin of holes and vividly connecting stars and cracks, then Golson jerked up stiffly in his seat and wrenched at his wheel convulsively. Skidding away to the left, the Morris narrowly missed the Viva, hit the bank, careered across the road and struck the other, then bounced back and went speeding diagonally towards the tree-lined base of the hill. In his rear vision mirror, McNally saw the car smash into an oak, tip up its boot and crash down again, then topple on to its side and burst into flames. He could see that the occupants hadn't got a hope of survival, but he didn't give a damn. A sense of fatalism possessed him. There was nothing for it but to go on to whatever the end must be. He was a victim: the victim of circumstances that his greed had brought into being. For all that had happened to him, and must happen to him, he could blame nobody but himself. There was a bitter satisfaction in that. He was the master of his fate, and the captain of his soul.

He kept the Viva speeding ahead. Now his mind thought coldly and objectively about the presence of the men in the Morris. They could only have been following Westmayne, but McNally was certain that the gang-boss would have left no instructions for them to do that. It looked to him as if the men might have called at Bellinger Place and met Gilda. She must have put them on to where they could find their boss, and given them some idea of what he had gone to do. A thing like that could only have been done with malice afore-thought. Gilda must have wanted to get rid of the men in a hurry, and at the same time to begin compromising Westmayne in their eyes. McNally couldn't explain what had happened otherwise. Everything pointed in one direction now. Gilda meant to grab the Lahkpore jewels and make a run for it on her own. He would have to reach her quickly or it would be too late.

McNally put the natural dangers of the winding roads out of his imagination. He fed the engine petrol. The needle swung around the speedometer and hovered over seventy. He kept dabbing at the brakes, and holding the wheel against the shrieking slide of his tyres. The miles sped by, and the scene under the sullen sky became less green and bleaker. The grey and pushful immensity of the sea seemed to thrust its image over the rain-torn horizon to the east.

Brow furrowed, McNally tried to make up his mind whether to go to Bellinger Place or the flat in Jutland Street. Then it occurred to him that Gilda wouldn't be at either. She, too, must have been wondering about the Police investigations that her relationship with him would inevitably have brought about. It followed that she would be afraid, in the event of Westmayne's slipping up in the attempt to kill him, that the threat his, McNally's, vengeance would represent would cause the Police to bring her under their protective eye. Equally, she would fear that, if the Police had Westmayne under surveillance, his, McNally's, murder, would be brought back to her door as the one person likely to have indicated his presence at Slack's Hole. No, Gilda wouldn't dare stay around her usual haunts with Westmayne on his way to a killing and the members of his gang following behind. Besides, McNally strongly doubted that Westmayne had hidden the genuine Lahkpore jewels in his home, normal place of business, or Gilda's flat. The risk of their discovery in any of those places would have remained too high. So where would he have hidden the loot? And where, by that same token, was the girl most likely to be found now?

Something vaguely remembered crept into McNally's mind. He had once heard Westmayne speak of Shangri-la, a beach house that he owned over towards Greystone Head. Westmayne had bragged about the number of girls whom he had seduced there across the years. By association, pretty girls and jewellery went together. It seemed a good bet that the loot had been concealed in the beach property. He would gamble on it anyhow. The change of direction would be helpful, too. He could approach Greystone Head without touching Eastport itself. That would eliminate all chance of getting picked up by the Police. Long before they had worked out which of Westmayne's three cars he was driving, he would have made a change of vehicle and probably be on his way with a fortune. The need for those protective walls no longer seemed quite so great.

Arriving at the next crossways, he turned left instead of going straight on. His road lifted and ran along the top of an embankment. He saw the broken mass of Eastport standing beyond shadowy waters that stirred from slight tidal influences and the action of wind swirls that carried rain across their surface. He let his right foot sink on to the floorboards. The Viva hurtled along at eighty plus, rocking slightly to the lift of air off the sodden camber. Its tyres sang in the rain.

Now the pattern of the fields lost its regularity over to the left. Farmhouses and cottages disappeared, and the coast-line came in sight, with the sudden lift of Greystone Head falling back into folded grass and woodlands, contours which were again topped at a distance by the blurring brown of curving cliffs and an angled glimpse of far off wavetops tossing under the murk.

Passing over another crossroads, McNally dipped on to a narrow and recently asphalted road which ribboned like a strip of polished liquorice towards the sea. He met no traffic; his reckless progress was in no way checked. Within two minutes he had reached the end of the road, turned left under a high, sandy bank covered by limp and blowing speargrass, and moved opposite the beach properties on the left of the coast road. Slowing a little, he watched the names painted on the little bungalows and huts as he passed, but he saw no sign of the one he sought. Then he rounded a bend, and moved into an area where Nature had sliced a deep wedge out of the terrain. Here he saw a sheltered dwelling, which was much larger and more ornate than most of those in the vicinity. This one carried the name Shangri-la painted over its front door, and Gilda's green Morris 1100 stood outside the gate. Elation filled him. His deductions had been correct, and the girl was still in the beach house.

McNally drove the Viva round the next bend, and stopped on the lay-by at the approaches to the climb over the back of Greystone Head. Switching off the engine, he got out of the car and began to scramble up the grassy slope on the landward side of the coast road. The climb was fairly demanding, and he collapsed weakly on his hands and knees at the top of it. He allowed himself a very short rest, then, with a palm pressed to his ribs, picked himself up and followed the descending ridge of high ground through a half-circle which brought him on to the incised land formation which contained Shangri-la.

Fully alert and checking his steps carefully, he descended towards the rear of the beach house. There he saw a small shed with its door standing open. He moved towards the shed with great care, fearing that Gilda might be inside, but an ear pressed to the wood told him that it was empty, and he rounded it on tip-toe and reached the house. Slinking to the nearest window in the rear wall, he squinted in at a corner of it, but saw only a bed and a few pieces of simple wooden furniture. Creeping to his right, he reached the back door, but, after pausing at it, side-stepped to a second window adjacent and peered through that also, seeing another bed and two or three more examples of the plain furniture. Satisfied that the rooms at the rear of the house were unoccupied, he returned to the back door and listened at it a moment, then turned the knob and added the pressure of his shoulder. The door gave inwards almost soundlessly, and he eased himself into the gap, lungs quivering and his tongue held between his teeth. A tiny dribble of sweat ran coldly away from his right temple. He inched into the house; then a sudden explosion of noise caused him to pull up short, his nerves jangling. Blinking, he got a grip on himself. It was all right. Gilda was using a hammer. Perhaps she was boxing up the loot.

He began to move again. A gloomy little passage ran before him for about nine feet, then made a ninety degree turn to the left. McNally neared the corner. Another burst of hammering dinned through the confined space. It sounded almost on top of him. Gilda couldn't be more than a few feet away. She was in for the surprise of her life.

McNally stepped into the continuation of the passage beyond the angle. He stood erect and absolutely still. He saw the girl kneeling under a small frosted window set in the wall behind her. She held a hammer in her right hand, and was banging away inexpertly at the ends of three loose floor boards. She was so engrossed in what she was doing that seconds passed before she became aware of his presence. Then she stiffened, jerked her head up, and met his eyes with so much shock that the hammer literally spilled away from her nerveless fingers and thudded to the boards. McNally gave her a nasty grin and said: 'Hello, sweetheart. You didn't expect to see me, did you?'

'Damn you, Dave!' Gilda muttered thickly, passing her knuckles across her moist forehead and leaving red marks in the unnatural whiteness of her skin.

'Damned I may be,' McNally taunted, 'but not dead. I'm still very much alive, my darling. I can't say the same for Gerry Westmayne.'

'You bastard!' she whispered.

'Or Piper, or Fairclough — or my old mate, Fred Golson.'

'You bastard!' she repeated, her teeth hardly parting and her lips beginning to tremble. 'Now for the grand slam?'

'Don't fret, honey,' he advised insidiously. 'I've decided not to kill you. Off and on, it's been on my mind to do you in, but that would be too simple and easy. You're a lovely girl, Gilda; a lovely lay. I expect you think, even if there's no fortune for you, you can go back to getting a good living out of mugs who pay for it. Sorry, my sweet; no more. I'm going to bash those fragile good looks of yours so badly that no man with half an eye in his head will ever want to look at you again.'

'You fiend!' she muttered thickly.

'You've got it right this time,' McNally

said. 'My ma wasn't too particular. My old man may've been the devil!' He enjoyed the way in which the girl shrank from him. It made up for much of the earlier suffering she had caused him, and restored his sense of manhood and power. 'Now, pretty face, let's see what you've got tucked under those planks.'

'Nothing!' Gilda declared, kneeling still, and her palms pressed hard to the floor.

He gazed into her ashen features. 'What the hell are you giving me?' he asked contemptuously. 'You've got the jewels down there, haven't you?'

'No. They were down there; but not now. They're in the next room. Look for yourself, Dave.'

McNally lunged at her, seized her by the tops of her arms, and hurled her into a doorway on the left. She crashed against the jamb, mouth and eyes agape, and her parted knees driven back towards her ears. She tried to scream, but only a mewing sound left her lips.

Bending down, McNally picked up the hammer. He thrust its iron tongue between two of the loose planks and ripped them up. Then, in a flurry of violent activity, he tore up the remainder of the floor with his bare hands and shrank back aghast from the hideously contorted features of the corpse that lay beneath. 'You bloody murderess!' he cried, blundering at Gilda with a hand raised. 'It's Teresa Sanderman! There's a smell of cyanide on her! You've poisoned her!'

15

McNally closed in as the girl cringed from him and began to back into the living-room behind her with a frantic movement of her hands and heels. He struck her as she started to rise, and she sprawled on her back, a hand to her reddened cheek and a sob trembling on her lips. 'You're a hundred times worse!' he declared. 'This killing was premeditated! Mine was forced on me!' Reaching down, he seized the blonde's chin and held it in crushing fingers. 'Why, Gilda?' he demanded. 'Why?'

'Mind your own business!' the girl lisped out truculently, her courage seeming to return as she realized that the sustained beating he had promised was not to begin yet.

McNally's eyes narrowed and his brow lined with thought. Gradually, understanding came and his expression lightened. 'She was your accomplice! You were mugging me, Westmayne — her — the lot of us from the start!'

'What if I was?' she asked disdainfully, her tones still garbled by the vice-like pressure of his hand about her mouth. 'Let go of me, you swine!'

He let go, throwing her backwards, and she glared up at him off her cocked elbows. 'Go on!' he ordered.

'You think you're so clever!' Gilda sneered. 'You don't know anything. Teresa and I used to be friends. She was on the game for a while after she lost her husband. She didn't blame me, when Westmayne pushed her out of his bed and asked me to join him instead. Teresa hated him; she didn't like being used. She knew all about the lust and selfishness of men. She wanted her revenge. That's when I saw how useful she could be.'

'No pauses!' McNally snapped.

'Still bullying, Dave?' the blonde asked vindictively. 'You were going to do so much; be such a big man. You thought I'd jump at the chance of sharing the goodies with you. You vain, silly man! I didn't want you or anybody like you. I'm remarkably self-sufficient. But money I need. Don't we all? Men are the providers; you know I accept that; so I was content to work on Gerry with what you'd blabbed to me — and leave him to do the providing; which he did, most adequately, yesterday.

'The robbery went like clockwork, didn't it? Gerry was full of himself; another great man. He phoned me to come to Shangri-la and look at the loot — which I did; and then we hid it under the boards in the passage. Sorry I was so niggardly with you yesterday evening, Dave; but I was expecting a heavy night with Westmayne — and I had to be at my best to lull his suspicions for what was due to happen in the morning.'

'You'd primed Teresa to ring the Police about the robbery at Westmayne's house during the night?'

'The linchpin,' Gilda agreed. 'I had to set in motion the train of events that would end at Slack's Hole. What did Brenner think of the fakes?'

'You certainly gambled, girl,' McNally

muttered, a whisper of reluctant admiration in his voice.

'Not so much as you might think, Dave. Work it through.'

'Was Teresa on a cut?'

'Of course. She was nobody's fool, you know. Revenge wasn't quite enough. But you didn't want any interruptions, did you, Dave? Now here you are, asking questions like mad.'

He shrugged. 'There's not much more to tell, is there? Where did the paste replicas come from?'

'The Hague. They were made by an expert who recently did some repairs on the Lahkpore State Jewels. Gerry Westmayne had some very good contacts; he was really a very able man. A far better man than you are, Dave.'

'That's why he's dead?'

Gilda gave a dry little laugh. 'Your luck must soon run out. It can't go on for ever.'

'No?' It was his turn to laugh. 'Next time you'll want to be my talisman.'

'You bumptious, semi-literate, crooked little bighead!' Gilda exclaimed, though her voice lacked real passion. 'I wouldn't spend another night with you for a king's ransom. You're a farmyard operative. Every bit the brute you claim you're not.'

McNally shuddered as he swallowed the words. He'd make her pay for them in a minute. But were they true?

She seemed to catch the thought. Her lips twisted, and her eyes mocked. 'It's true. Ask some of the other girls.'

The colour rose into McNally's face, and he felt shame choke in his throat. The bitch had won; his ego had split from top to bottom. 'Where are the jewels?' he choked.

'On the floor at the other side of the table.'

He became aware of the contents of the living-room now. Of the big dining table, of the wax fruits that gleamed in a Chinese bowl on the sideboard, of the brass sea-clock on the wall, of the cocktail cabinet on the left of the fireplace, and the cut-glass decanter and glasses that glittered on a tray on the windowseat. He moved around the table and saw the Maharajah's silver jewel casket standing on the carpet. Opening the lid, he gazed down upon the gems that flashed and scintillated within. He was satisfied. Even now he might fulfill his dreams.

'Drink?' Gilda asked, pouring a whisky from the decanter and holding out the glass. 'Never beat up a girl cold sober.'

Amazement, disdain, anger, and amusement passed over McNally's features. 'Don't make me laugh! I'm not trusting Teresa!'

Gilda shrugged, and sipped from the glass, her eyes coldly amused. Then she went to the cocktail cabinet and took a cigarette from a box lying on top of it. 'There are some matches in my handbag,' she said, nodding to where the hated bag stood on the mantelpiece.

'Get 'em yourself.'

This time only one of her shoulders lifted and fell, and she sauntered to the mantelpiece and lifted the flap of the bag, taking out a matchbox, which she rattled by her ear. 'Cigarette?' she asked, lighting her own and exhaling pleasurably.

'You're a cool customer now,' McNally observed, walking to the box on the cocktail cabinet and helping himself to a cigarette. 'Don't put the matches up.'

But she already had. 'I don't think you'll hurt me, Dave,' she purred, smiling her most seductive smile as she took the bag off the mantelpiece and put her hand inside it.

'Won't I hell!' he exclaimed, raising the cigarette towards his lips. 'Hearts and roses again. I thought you were smarter.' He listened to her thrilling simper, but there was no response from his blood. And then light from the window flashed minutely off the crystals half buried in the tobacco which was about to touch his lips. He stopped the movement, startled, then, with a grunt of horror, threw the cigarette from him and yelled: 'You wicked hellcat! So that's how you did it!'

Murder glared from the blonde's eyes. Her hand reappeared from the handbag. This time it held a .22 automatic instead of a box of matches. The weapon cracked at McNally twice, and he was aware of a double impact that caused the room to spin and darken. Then the floor rushed up to meet him, and he seemed to merge with it in a terrible concussion. He lay utterly still, his mind still functioning in a mental twilight, but his body apparently dead.

Then he was dimly aware of Gilda bending over him. He expected her to put the gun to his ear and finish him off. But she appeared satisfied that he was dead. Straightening, she turned away and picked up the jewel casket. He heard her wrap it in a cloth of some sort and carry it to the building's front door. After that, she went outside and closed up behind her with a bang that suggested sudden haste.

McNally heard the Moris 1100 start up, make a threepoint turn, and go speeding away towards the town. He made a titanic effort to get his body working again. It would be all too easy to lie there and wait for his life to ebb away. He was going to die, yes; but not before he had finished what he must now do. He felt a spasmodic tingling in his nerves and muscles. His sight cleared a good deal. A minimal energy returned. He managed to raise himself, grip the edge of the table, and force himself upright. Holding on wherever he could, he tottered to the front door and opened it. Rain blew in upon his face; the chill revived him still further. He staggered to the garden gate, turned on to the road, and shuffled off towards the lay-by on which he had left the Viva. Reason told him that he had no chance of catching Gilda now. She would be miles away before he could set out in pursuit. But he didn't care a jot for reason. He would catch up with Gilda; he knew it with a certainty too complete for words. How it would happen, he couldn't say. Destiny knew its business.

He reached the Viva and opened the driver's door. Crouching inside, he dropped into the seat behind the wheel and drew his legs after him. There was blood all over his chest; it smothered the controls as he set the vehicle into motion; but he felt no pain — just a leaden numbness. Then he realized that the car was jumping and bucking on a half engaged clutch. He raised his left knee an inch or two and, as the erratic motion flattened out, tugged feebly at the wheel and tried to make a full right turn; but the bonnet didn't come round quickly enough and he bumped into the opposite verge, jarring himself rather badly. Blinking and gasping, he groped about in the box to find reverse. Eventually the truant gear engaged, and he shot backwards across the road and bumped into a concrete refuse container on the side of the lay-by. Then, after more groping and grinding with the gear-stick, he bucked forward again and arced towards the white line, getting himself hooted and sworn at by the driver of a twelve-wheeler which happened to be heading for Eastport at that moment.

Indifferent to bad language and scowling faces, McNally completed his turn and set off in the lorry's wake, his control over the accelerator a very limited one. Swinging out, he overtook the twelve-wheeler on the first bend, earning himself another spate of furious hooting and invective, fought his way out of a screeching slide, his blunt and slippery fingers clawing, then straightened up as he passed Shangri-la and hurtled between beach and banks at seventy. The road camber tilted towards the sea. He raised his speed to eighty. Water reared out of puddles and lashed his windscreen. He touched the verge, went into a short vicious skid, saw the sea and the town snake wildly, converge, and come hurtling at him, but his touch was charmed, and his tyres held him only inches short of disaster. Risks meant nothing any more; narrow escapes were a jest. The speedo needle touched top speed and hung.

McNally saw cars ahead: a line of them running up to an intersection beyond the yacht basin. The way into town was completely blocked by a low-loader which had broken down while hauling a massive piece of machinery. McNally slowed down, and braked to a shuddering stop, near the crown of the road and just behind the last vehicle in the line of delayed traffic. It came as no surprise to him when he saw Gilda's Morris among the leaders of the queue. Destiny had fixed things. Gilda now had no more hope than he. Tonight they would both be dead. There would be no stars in their darkness; and the darkness would be without end.

He watched and waited, listening to the blood that dripped from him to the floor. Two huge crawlers appeared up front. Chains were fetched out, and the workmen by the low-loader attached the tractors to it, signalled to the driver of the transport that all was well, then urged the men on the crawlers to move ahead. Slowly, the low-loader and its burden were towed away from the intersection and the traffic from both directions was restored to free flow.

The Viva roared into motion. McNally pulled out, regardless of approaching cars, and bored forward, zigzagging crazily in his efforts to catch up with the Morris 1100. He grazed one oncoming vehicle, and caused two others to collide. Horns screeched at him, fists wagged, and eyes glared in panic. A policeman jumped into his path then, just as hurriedly, jumped out of it again. He snaked between a braking Renault and its attendant Peugeot, and came out with Gilda's car just in front of him. He got ready to pull across the front of the Morris and cut it off, but Gilda, obviously well aware that something extraordinary had been happening in her wake, appeared to catch a glimpse of his face in her rear vision mirror. Then she craned at him, her eyes full of fright, and sent her car shooting to the front.

The machines sped along the promenade. McNally used every manoeuvre he could think of to place himself in a position to overtake. He even tried passing along the wrong side of the islands and lampstandards in an effort to find an opening through which he could lance back and force the girl to a standstill. But by counter-moves and sheer speed she managed to keep ahead.

They were nearing the Keystone Pier when she played him at his own game. Braking back almost to a halt, she clashed the gears and skidded sharply to the right, passing between two islands and picking up a road that led into the town, while he raced onwards and lost valuable seconds in treading on his brakes and coming about. But he recovered quickly, gunned his motor as he neared the road along which the green Morris had disappeared, broadsided on to it, lurched over a curb, straightened through another hissing of rubber and steam, and rocketed away in full pursuit again, the receding Morris still just in view.

Knifing through the traffic, he caught up fast. A road junction loomed. The girl passed over it, without looking left or right, and entered the heart of the town. McNally followed without losing an inch of ground. Now he was literally hanging on the other car's rear bumper. He was aware that vehicles on both sides of the street were braking hard to keep clear of the pursuit. Huge plate-glass windows threw back images of the chase. McNally caught a glimpse of his own face, corpselike and swimming behind the shadows in the glass, and then of Gilda's, white and vicious, with the lips drawn back against the teeth. Neither was going to give; neither was going to break. The pursuit went on at sixty.

Up front a set of traffic lights showed amber, and then they turned red. Gilda went over them. McNally did the same, almost hitting a police car that had its blue light flashing. From the corner of his eye, he saw the vehicle jerk to a stop and its occupants pitch forward. In the same split second, he also saw Blessingay's face, lips parted and eyes accusing, and knew the chief inspector would be in at the end. That would be fitting, of course.

Then McNally gave himself up to the chase again. It was evident now that Gilda was heading for the river. Narrow streets closed in upon them; but as the cars twisted and turned. McNally guessed what the girl intended. She was too clever to leave anything to chance. He felt sure she had a boy friend waiting somewhere at the quayside with a launch. The poor mug probably planned to drop her off on the Continent, and collect his reward. McNally could imagine how Gilda would enjoy double-crossing whoever it was. But it would never be.

Pure desperation possessed the girl now. She ran in and out of almost impossible places, hitting a wall in cornering, lurching over the wheel of a fallen bicycle, and passing between lines of railway waggons where iron tracks ran toward the quay. McNally stayed with her. He sensed the mounting throb of fury and panic in the girl. She was near the end of her tether.

Now they ran out into the open. A broad street stretched before them towards the river. McNally again clocked eighty. He drew level with the Morris, and inched over, forcing the green car nearer and nearer to a warehouse wall. He expected the blonde to brake to a stop: she appeared to have no alternative, with the river and an impossible lefthand bend directly ahead; but she again went to top speed and brushed out of the gap between the wall and the Viva. Drawing ahead, she swung out and attempted the acute turn on to the quayside road, but her locking wheels met a thick patch of oil and she skidded into the corner of the warehouse, rode up and rocked away in collision, with glass and wreckage flying off the car, then turned over and spun across the quay, bursting into flames as she curved through empty air and plunged towards the river.

His reflexes gone, McNally tried to pull up as his Viva shot across the quay; but his brakes came on too late and the front of his car smashed into a huge iron bollard. The impact burst the doors open, and he was flung out and went cartwheeling into a pile of empty boxes which stood nearby. These erupted about him, and left him lying twisted and broken in their midst.

He lay staring at the sky, for how long he didn't know, and an incredible weakness filled him. Then a face appeared above his own. 'Hello, Chief Inspector,' he murmured.

'Hello, lad,' Blessingay said. 'Rum go, eh?'

'Yes. All for nothing.'

'It always is. What did you hope to get out of it?'

McNally smiled a little, surprised that the question need be asked. 'A place in the sun,' he said — 'a Mercedes.' Then his head rolled on to his shoulder, and he quietly died.

Blessingay pressed a hand to the

middle of his back, and slowly straightened up. He turned to Sergeant Logan, who had been standing between the dead man and the patrol car at the edge of the quay. 'Nice job!' he growled. 'It's my guess we'll find the real Lahkpore jewels lying on the bottom with the girl. We'll send a diver down.'

Logan nodded. 'What did he say, sir?' he asked curiously.

'I asked him what he had really hoped to get out of it. He said a place in the sun — and a Mercedes.' Blessingay shook his head regretfully, and moved back towards the patrol car. 'No Mercedes, I'm afraid. It's a hearse for McNally.'

THE END

Other titles in the
Linford Mystery Library:

THE SISKIYOU TWO-STEP

Richard Hoyt

John Denson, a private investigator, goes to Oregon's North Umpqua River to fish trout but, instead, he finds himself caught up in a net of international intelligence agents and academics. It all starts when the naked body of a girl with a bullet hole between her eyes goes rushing past Denson in the rapids. He embarks on a bizarre search to find the girl's identity and to bring her killer to justice. Strange clues lead to three more corpses, and only the Siskiyou Two-Step saves Denson from being the fourth . . .

THREE MAY KEEP A SECRET

Stella Phillips

The proudest citizens of Dolph Hill would not deny that it was a backwater where nothing ever happened — until, that is, the arrival of handsome, secretive Peter Markland disturbs the surface. After his shocking and violent death, old secrets begin to emerge. Detectives Matthew Furnival and Reg King are put on the case. As they delve through the conflicting mysteries, how will they arrive at the one relevant truth?

SHERLOCK HOLMES: THE WAY OF ALL FLESH

Daniel Ward

Sherlock Holmes is called in to investigate when the body of an Italian diplomat is discovered in the River Thames, his torso horrifically mutilated. Fearing the political repercussions — the diplomat being in London to initiate talks regarding a secret naval treaty between the two nations — the Government entrust Holmes with the delicate task of uncovering the truth behind the brutal murder. Events take a shocking turn, however, when a young solicitor is found slain in the East End, his body similarly mutilated . . .

THE LIGHT BENDERS

John Newton Chance

Can incoming metals from outer space bring in contamination that can kill mankind? Are rockets safe from picking up invading germs? The V2 rocket has been lost in the midst of its own desolation for nearly thirty years when a piece of its metal comes into the hands of the only occupier of the bomb site. Then suddenly the metal starts to come alive, to write, to scream, to terrify the holder and the man who had come to find out why this whole deserted place had somehow gathered to itself the mark of Cain . . .

CONFESS TO DR. MORELLE

Ernest Dudley

A pretty girl and a drunken producer are involved in a dramatic motor accident on the road from Lyons to Paris — a fruitful source for black-mail. The first sinister consequence occurs at a party where, among the actresses and producers, Dr. Morelle is present with his secretary, Miss Frayle. The famous criminologist finds himself plunged into one of the strangest cases of his career as he takes to the airwaves to unmask a murderer before he can kill again!